“I think we’re being followed,” Nick said.

“That’s a Las Sombras guy. He’s tailing us.” Nick directed his next sentence to the deputy. “I wouldn’t be surprised if he tries to force us off the road.”

The deputy’s gaze locked with Nick’s. “What are they after?”

“Us. They know I’m a cop and they think I have their missing drugs. They’re going to do anything they can to get me. Including pinning the murder of federal agents on me.”

“He’s gaining on us,” Alexis said, bracing for impact.

The car made contact with the police cruiser. Metal crunched and they swerved on the road.

The car raced toward them and made contact with the rear of their vehicle again. The impact shoved them forward.

“We’re going to lose control,” the deputy yelled.

The car left the road and began to roll down the embankment.

Alexis’s screams drowned out the crunching of metal and breaking of glass…

Jennifer Pierce lives in Arkansas, where she's busy raising two children and a husband. She's a paralegal by trade and an author by free time. She's fluent in sarcasm and *Princess Bride* quotes. Her love of books began with trips to the library with her grandmother. Please don't ask her to name her favorite book—it's like trying to pick her favorite child. And unicorns. She loved unicorns before they were cool.

Books by Jennifer Pierce

Love Inspired Suspense

Colorado Double Cross

Visit the Author Profile page at LoveInspired.com.

Colorado Double Cross

JENNIFER PIERCE

Recycling programs for this product may not exist in your area.

ISBN-13: 978-1-335-59803-5

Colorado Double Cross

Love Inspired
22 Adelaide St. West, 41st Floor
Toronto, Ontario M5H 4E3, Canada
www.LoveInspired.com

Printed in Lithuania

And have no fellowship with the unfruitful works of darkness, but rather reprove them.

—*Ephesians* 5:11

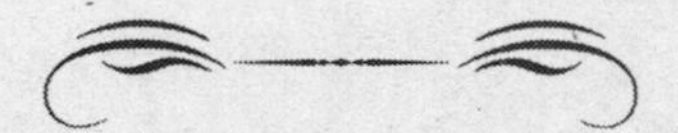

To my friends and family,
thank you for your love and support.
To Lisa, thank you for helping make my dream come true.

ONE

Blood trickled down Nick Anderson's face from a cut above his left eye. Courtesy of Matthias, one of the Las Sombras enforcers. Nick knew going undercover in the drug cartel would be dangerous and there would be a chance that his cover as a DEA agent could be blown, but he'd hoped it would never happen.

He'd been undercover for almost a year. But he wasn't going home until he found out who killed his partner.

Matthias's meaty fist connected with Nick's jaw this time. Pain radiated through his head. He barely took a breath before Matthias punched him in the stomach.

"We know who you are and what you've done." Matthias spit in Nick's face. "Traitor. You think you can get away with being a cop and stealing our drugs?"

Nick wanted to wipe his face. And Matthias's too—on the cement floor. But he couldn't, since his hands were occupied trying to free themselves from the restraints holding them behind the chair. That and the exhaustion weighing him down.

He took a deep breath. "I don't know what you think you know. But you're wrong."

Except Matthias wasn't completely wrong, was he? They knew Nick was law enforcement but did they know he was DEA? He wasn't about to confess to being an undercover DEA agent. Deny, deny, deny. And maybe then he'd live to see tomorrow.

"You're a cop." Matthias landed another punch. This time

to Nick's temple, causing his vision to blur. "And now a major shipment is missing."

"A cop? That's hilarious." Nick chuckled, squeezed his eyes shut and shook his head. The missing drugs were new information to him. "What makes you think that?"

"We don't *think*. We *know*. And once you tell us what we want, I'm going to enjoy teaching you a lesson."

"Where are you getting your information?" Nick asked through gritted teeth.

He wasn't sure how his cover had been blown, or how he'd been blamed for the missing drugs, but now was not the time to worry about it. He moved his wrists, attempting to loosen the ropes. It was no use; the knots were tight.

"Who are you working for?" Matthias threw another punch. This time his fist connected with Nick's lip, filling his mouth with a metallic taste.

So, they knew he was a cop but not what agency. Maybe that could play in his favor.

Nick turned his head to the side and spit. "I didn't take those drugs. When I find out who's filling your head with lies, I'm going to have to set them straight."

Nick had to play the tough guy, redirect Matthias's attention. Learn as much as he could. The more he knew, the more ammo he had to bring Las Sombras down. Bring the culprit to justice and make the whole cartel pay for his partner Tony's death. Of course, Nick blamed himself for Tony's death. If he had taken Tony's concerns more seriously, maybe he'd still be alive. But Nick wasn't the one that had forced Tony's car off the road. Someone else was responsible for that and Nick was convinced it was someone in the cartel.

"Oh. Look at you, tough guy." Matthias used both hands and tipped the chair over, sending it falling backward.

Nick's head hit the cement floor with a thud that echoed

in his ears. Nausea roiled. As his head started to clear, the pain in his hands began to register. They were wedged between the chair and the floor.

Matthias began kicking him in the ribs. Pain shot through Nick's torso. Each kick hurting worse than the last.

"That's enough, Matthias," Felipe Benitez, the head of Las Sombras, said, standing in the doorway.

Matthias took several steps back, giving Felipe room to enter. He unbuttoned his suit jacket and crouched beside Nick.

"How's it going, Nico?" Felipe threw his own punch. "Sit him up."

Matthias grabbed Nick by the shirt collar and lifted the chair upright. Matthias was a big man and insanely strong. Perfect for an enforcer. The fact that he enjoyed inflicting pain didn't hurt either.

Did you kill my partner? Nick wondered.

"Nico, I've got some missing merchandise." Felipe pulled a handkerchief from his suit pocket and wiped the blood from his knuckles. "And I've heard a terrible rumor about you." Felipe tossed the handkerchief to the ground, leaned against the wall and studied Nick with the dark stare of a man who had seen evil up close—and ordered it done. "Or do you prefer Nick Anderson?"

Nick kept his face neutral. Careful to give no recognition to his real identity. "It's Nico. I don't know who Nick Anderson is."

"Are you sure? You look an awful lot like him." Felipe stared at him.

Nick wasn't going to squirm under the intensity. "Must be a doppelgänger because I'm pretty sure the ID in my pocket says Nico Andrews."

"It doesn't really matter what your name is. Just tell me

where my merchandise is, and I'll make your death swift and relatively pain free."

"And what if I don't? Seeing as you've got the wrong guy and all."

"I won't beg. But you will." Felipe pulled a hunting knife from a sheath on his hip.

Movement at the window behind Felipe caught Nick's eye.

A woman stared through the window. All he could see was a knit cap and her eyes. The same knit cap he'd seen on the woman sneaking around earlier. He'd been on his way to confront her when Matthias had clobbered him from behind.

Who was she and why was she here? Did she have anything to do with why he was tied to the chair?

"Which leg do you want it in first?" Felipe growled as he waved the knife.

The woman's face disappeared. Hopefully, she'd seen enough and was hightailing it out of here. Las Sombras weren't people to mess with. And when Nick got free, he'd be asking her a few questions if she was still around.

Felipe stepped forward, raised his arm and brought it down quickly. Nick braced himself for the pain.

A howl came from inside the building.

Alexis White slowly backed away from the window. What had she been thinking? She hadn't been. She was a Realtor, not a crime fighter. But the chance to prove she was right and get justice moved her feet despite the danger. She wasn't made for this. She wasn't strong and fearless. No one but her believed the car accident that ended her husband's life was more than just an accident. The DEA, and the police, just dismissed her claims that it was an intentional act to end her and Tony's lives by running them off the road.

Now he was dead, and she was broken. The need to prove

everyone wrong, to prove the accident was intentional, had fueled her recovery and pushed her forward. Then she'd found Tony's notes in the cabin. Schematics of a compound conveniently located a couple miles down the mountain from the hunting cabin he'd bought in Dean, Colorado, before he died. There were notes about weaknesses to the compound. Entrances and exits. Times and dates. Nothing she understood.

She'd thought about turning the notes over to the DEA, but they hadn't believed his death was intentional. And considering before his death Tony had been afraid there was a mole in the agency, she would need more information before going to the police. Now, finding Tony's killer was the reason she was alive.

It was why she was here, facing down a cartel. Trying to avenge her husband and put his killers behind bars.

Alexis inhaled deeply through her nose and pushed the fear away. She wasn't going to back down or get distracted from her purpose. *You can do this.*

Months ago there was one person who had believed her. At least she'd thought he had, because it seemed like he listened. But then he'd disappeared, like everyone else who should've stood by her.

Now it had been almost a year since the accident and she hadn't seen Tony's partner since he'd visited her in the hospital right after the accident. He hadn't even attended the funeral. The fact that Nick had looked similar to that man in the window was just wishful thinking. He was probably dead just like her husband.

No, it was her fault Tony was dead. She'd opened her mouth and told the wrong person about Tony's concerns about a mole in the agency and he'd paid with his life. She took a deep breath to steady herself. She'd come too far to quit now. Proving who killed Tony would help absolve the guilt that plagued her.

Right?

Alexis walked with soft footsteps to the edge of the building. Where should she go? Obviously, the man tied to the chair was in danger, but what could she do about it? She was outnumbered and she'd left her gun at the cabin.

This walk onto Las Sombras land hadn't been a part of today's plan. Maybe she could create a distraction, lure the captors away from the building and free the man. But he was also a Las Sombras. Would self-preservation outweigh his loyalty to them? Or would she just be walking herself into danger?

She was pretty certain the man had spotted her and was on his way to confront her when he'd been attacked from behind. She was given a chance to escape. Yet here she was in the middle of the compound. Maybe if she saved him, he'd think he owed her a debt. She could use that to get him to turn on Las Sombras. They obviously didn't want him anymore.

She peeked around the building. There was another structure across a single-lane road identical to the building she was hiding by. Several metal cans were standing haphazardly at the corner. She could knock them over and hide. They'd start searching and she could sneak in the building and free the man.

Her head was yanked back by her ponytail, and she let out a yelp as her body stumbled back.

"What do we have here?" Hot putrid breath washed over the side of her face as one of the Las Sombras men looked over her shoulder.

Dread filled her. She'd spent too much time thinking and wallowing in guilt, and not enough time running.

The man let go of her ponytail and grabbed her upper arm in a viselike grip. "Since you want to know what's going on in there, why don't I just take you to join the fun?" He yanked her through the door.

The building didn't look like much on the outside and the inside was just as decrepit. He dragged her through a room stacked with boxes, down a narrow hallway and into a smaller room. The man she'd seen through the window was still seated in the chair. His left eye was swollen and starting to bruise. What would have been a neat beard, if not for his encounter in this room, covered the bottom of his face. They were going to do to her what they'd done to him.

"Look who I found snooping around outside."

She was shoved to the center of the room. Her body trembled. She hadn't thought through everything.

The man with the knife closed in on her. "Who are you?" He studied her face. Then peered behind her to where the man in the chair was. "She with you, Nico?"

Nico didn't respond; he just stared at the suited man.

"Your silence speaks volumes. You do know her." The suited man came and stood next to her and twirled the hair in her ponytail.

"I don't know that man!" she screeched.

"Yet you were found peeking in the one window where Nico was being held. This is a large compound—doesn't seem too coincidental to me," the man snarled.

She gulped. It was coincidental, but he'd never believe it.

"Maybe a girlfriend." He yanked her ponytail, pulling her head back and exposing her neck. Something cold traced from one side of her neck to the other. "It'd be a shame if I slipped and cut her."

Her breath hitched as something pricked her neck. Her heart beat rapidly in her chest.

"I don't know her." The voice belonging to Nico was oddly familiar. But that was impossible. She didn't know him.

"You know I'm not inclined to believe you. Not when

you've been lying to us this whole time," the man with the knife snarled.

"Okay, believe what you want, but why kill her? You know we're always needing help on the cutting floor. With all the overdoses. Put her to work," Nico said with a tone of indifference.

He was being flippant with her life. How could someone be so callous? Tears burned her eyes. She wasn't going to give them the satisfaction of seeing her cry. Alexis's neck and shoulders hurt from being forced to look up. Anxiety gnawed at her chest. Was she going to die here? Her body tossed away like trash? She gulped the scream that was working its way up her throat.

Her ponytail was released and she was shoved to the ground, landing on her injured hip. The injury she received in the car wreck that killed Tony. A cry escaped her mouth as pain radiated down her leg.

"Nico, you claim to be loyal to Las Sombras. How about you prove it? Kill two birds with one stone. Or a nosy bird with a knife at least. Then we'll talk about my missing merchandise."

"You want me to do the dirty work so you can keep your hands clean." Nico shrugged. "Sure, let's do this."

Nausea roiled in her stomach. She was going to be sick. They were talking so casually about killing her.

No. She wasn't going to die here. Not like this. She didn't know who'd killed Tony, but somehow, she got the feeling she was closer than ever right now to learning the truth.

Lord, don't let me die before I find out. Her faith was rusty since his death. But there was no one else to cry out to.

She jumped to her feet and ran for the hall. She wasn't fast enough. The man who'd found her grabbed her around the waist and lifted her off the ground. She screamed and kicked her legs wildly despite the pain in her hip and leg.

She aimed for the man's knees or groin, trying to incapacitate him.

"Stop squirming," the man said through gritted teeth before dropping her on the ground. She stood up. A fist made contact with her cheek. The room started to spin before everything went black.

Nick fought with everything inside him not to react. He'd thought the woman had looked familiar but it wasn't until he saw her up close that he knew exactly who she was. Alexis White. Tony's wife.

What was she doing here? His job just got twice as hard. Now he was responsible for the safety of a civilian. Not just any civilian. His partner's wife. The same partner he'd failed by sending him into this mess—the one whose death he was responsible for.

And now he was responsible for her life.

Giving Felipe any hint that Nick knew Alexis would tip the balance in Las Sombras's favor. Not that they really believed him anyway.

Alexis crumpled at his feet.

"Thank you." Nick blew out a breath. "Her screaming was hurting my ears."

Make jokes and stall. Nick was able to see two people in the room but there was no telling how many were milling about beyond the door. He could disarm these guys, get Alexis and make a run for it. That was if Alexis woke up. If not, he'd have to carry her out.

Could he do it? The wound in his leg screamed in pain, so running would definitely be troublesome. He couldn't be sure the kicks he'd taken to the ribs hadn't broken one or two. He took a deep breath, gauging his lung capacity. Pain shot through his chest. At least cracked, if not broken. He'd had worse.

"So, Nico. Are you Nico or are you Nick?" Felipe questioned.

"Why don't you untie me to find out." Nick balled his fists. "Give me the knife. I'll dispatch the girl and we can move on, find your merchandise and put who really belongs in this chair in it."

Felipe produced a gun from inside his blazer and aimed it square at Nick's chest. Adrenaline coursed through him. He hadn't been convincing enough. He'd let Tony—and now Alexis as well—down.

Alexis would be left in the hands of Las Sombras. An evil no one should have to encounter. Yet Tony had, and still kept his faith in God. A God Nick had never known. Tony had stared down the face of evil many times and still believed there was a good and gracious God. Nick had envied him that. Did Alexis share his faith? Would that faith be enough to carry her through whatever Las Sombras had planned for her?

Guilt racked Nick's chest. There was nothing he could do to protect her from a bleak and painful future at the hands of Las Sombras. He'd already clouded her life with misery when he let Tony die.

"Untie him, Matthias," Felipe instructed.

The air whooshed from Nick's lungs. There was still a chance he could save Alexis and himself.

Matthias advanced on him and delivered another punch to the gut.

"Matthias," Felipe reprimanded.

Matthias grunted as he rounded the chair and started untying Nick's hands. As the ropes were loosened, the ache in Nick's muscles lessened. He pulled his hands in front of him and shook them, allowing the blood to flow as the vascular system had intended. His fingers tingled as they regained feeling.

"On with it." Felipe tossed the knife and it clanged at Nick's feet. "Kill her."

"Can I get a moment to regain use of my hands? If you hadn't noticed they've been behind my back and wedged between the chair and the cement for a while." Nick opened and closed his fists. Stalling for time.

Time to plan, and time for Alexis to wake up. He wasn't ignorant; he knew he was as good as dead once he did what they asked and killed Alexis. Not that he was going to do that.

Nick was going to get them both out of this.

He bent over and picked up the knife. "All right, let's get this show on the road." He limped over to Alexis's still body and squatted down. "Okay, sleeping beauty, time to wake up. So you can die." He reached to roll her over. She moved a little. He shook her and hissed, "Alexis?"

She whirled her face to stare at him, eyes wide in panic.

He pinched the blade between his forefinger and thumb. "Get ready to run," he whispered.

He stood and threw the knife.

Felipe hit the ground and the gun skittered across the dilapidated wood floor. He grabbed the knife protruding from his thigh. "You're going to pay for that."

A thigh for a thigh.

Matthias lunged for the gun. Nick tackled him at the waist and flipped Matthias to his back. Both of them sprawled on the ground. Matthias kicked and jabbed at him.

Where was Felipe? Time was of the essence; Nick needed to get to the gun before Felipe did. A solid punch to Matthias's head had him out cold.

Felipe was dragging himself toward the gun. Nick scrambled up and hobbled over to the gun.

"Not so fast." Nick picked up the gun and aimed it at Felipe.

"Traitor," Felipe spit.

"Just remember, I could have killed you. But I didn't. You have the wrong guy. I don't have your drugs. You'll see." Nick leveled a steely glare at the man. He needed Felipe to think he was acting out of self-preservation to remain alive and involved in the cartel. Not to bring the cartel down.

Nick looked at Alexis. "We've got to go." He grabbed her arm and pulled her to a standing position.

"Don't touch me." She threw a punch, landing a fairly good uppercut to his jaw. His teeth clattered together. She turned and dashed out of the room ahead of him.

"Wait!" He didn't want to use her name where Felipe could hear. Right now she was still unknown to them. Nick wanted to keep it that way as long as possible.

Did she know where she was going? He followed her down the hall.

She burst through the door and headed left.

"Alexis, wait," he yelled. He'd used her name earlier and she'd responded to it but she wasn't now. Didn't she know who he was?

Two Las Sombras guys stepped out of the building across the dirt road. Nick aimed his gun and fired two quick shots but more Las Sombras were coming. Soon enough the whole cartel would be on their tails.

He had to lead them away from Alexis. Nick took off in the opposite direction.

The moon was full but its light was hindered by the canopy of leaves in the forest.

Nick navigated the terrain by memory and instinct. His lungs screamed for oxygen despite the pain slicing through his rib cage, and his heart beat like it would burst through his chest while his legs were weak with strain. He was in shape and a run shouldn't be affecting him this much but his body had taken a beating and the wound in his thigh was slowing him down.

Death had been imminent until Alexis was caught snooping around the compound. They would have killed him if she hadn't been discovered. Right now, he owed her his life, and that meant protecting her with every skill he had and all the drive he'd put into finding Tony's killer.

Nick fired two shots into the ground, to make sure the Las Sombras guys followed him and not Alexis, then jammed the gun into his waistband and ran in the direction of the road. As long as she got away, that was what mattered. That she lived. He couldn't be responsible for the death of another person because he'd failed. Again.

Nick had studied maps of the area before moving into the Las Sombras compound in the Colorado mountains and remembered seeing a hunting cabin a couple miles along the road to the north of the compound—the place Tony had told him about. The one he'd bought to keep tabs on the cartel. The DEA had been watching Las Sombras for a while and Tony was lead on the case, but he'd become obsessed with it and used his own money and time to do further investigations.

Nick just needed to make it to the cabin, where he could hide out undetected until he could figure out who to trust. Unless of course it was occupied. Had Alexis sold it after Tony's death? The thought of Las Sombras catching up to him propelled him farther. The cabin's occupancy was the least of his concerns right now. He'd deal with that when he got there.

His foot caught a tree root and he crashed to the ground, hitting his knee on something hard. Pain radiated up and down his leg as the smell of damp earth filled his nose. He lay on the forest floor and listened for sounds of a pursuit. The silent forest gave him no hope. He knew these guys, had lived with them for a year. They were well trained. Hunters. And he was their prey.

He should just lie here, let them catch him. It would be his penance for Tony's death. He knew now Tony had been right all along, and that his death no longer seemed like a tragic accident. It wasn't that Nick hadn't believed Tony when he'd said he thought there was a mole in the agency. It was more that he didn't want to believe it.

Nick's conscience wouldn't let him give up now. Las Sombras had hurt too many people and needed to be brought down. If he died, then so did the DEA's case. They'd have to start over with a new undercover agent.

Now he knew that Alexis was out there somewhere as well.

He stood and took a tentative step, and more pain radiated throughout his leg. He pushed through. If he stopped, this would be a walk in the park compared to the pain Las Sombras would cause. Stumbling, he caught himself on a tree before he fell. The road should be close by; he'd run at least two miles, hadn't he?

A gunshot sounded behind him.

They were closing in. He reached for the gun in his waistband to shoot some wild shots to hopefully slow them down a bit, but the gun was gone. He must have lost it in the fall and there was no time to search for it. Adrenaline filled his veins and he pressed on. They were close enough to wound him. It would slow him down, and they'd catch him. Back at the compound again they'd take their time torturing him for betraying them and for the location of the drugs. Thanks to Felipe, each step was agonizing. He wouldn't last much longer on his injured leg.

What would he do once he reached the road? He'd be able to move quicker with the terrain evening out but so would his pursuers. He wasn't going to make it out of this alive. He'd never be able to outrun them in his injured state.

Defeat started settling on his shoulders and then he broke through a clearing of trees and his foot hit asphalt. Bright lights from his left blinded him. There was no time to dart back into the woods. He was caught.

TWO

Alexis closed the driver's door quietly and walked softly to the front of the vehicle, as she didn't want to spook an already injured animal. Had she really hit something? Or someone?

She had run through the dense forest and headed straight to the road where she'd parked the car. After selling their home and moving into the secluded hunting cabin Tony had bought, she'd gotten to know this mountain road well. Tony loved hunting and had always told her stories about motorists being surprised by deer or other wild animals jumping out of the dense forest and totaling their vehicles. After finding the notes about the Las Sombras compound and how there might be a mole in the agency, Alexis had doubted the cabin purchase was just about hunting. Another check in the married-to-the-job column. It seemed like there were more checks in that than in the married-to-Alexis column.

A dark shape had darted out in front of her SUV and she'd smashed her foot on the brake in enough time to keep from hitting the animal or person. Whatever it was had then slumped out of sight.

Low moaning came from the ground just out of her line of sight. That wasn't an animal.

Her pace quickened. She came around the front bumper and found the man from the building lying in the road. What had they called him? Nico?

He'd known her name.

That meant Las Sombras knew who she was. Which meant she should leave this bad guy—one of them—here.

She had to live to fight another day, to get justice for her husband.

But for some reason, she just couldn't leave.

This man, whoever he was, had saved her life.

He lay on his back. Blood streamed from a cut across his forehead that would require stitches and he was bleeding from the wound to his leg. How badly had he been beaten? He could have internal injuries and possible spinal injuries. Even though she never finished medical school, thanks to Las Sombras, her medical school knowledge kicked in. His sweat-and-blood-smeared face was bruised. His bottom lip was swollen and blood was crusted on his beard. Those were the same wounds he had in the room. She didn't see any fresh wounds.

He moved and started to stand.

"You need an ambulance." She winced. The man looked worse after his run through the woods.

"There's no time. We need to get out of here."

She'd heard gunfire after she'd escaped the building. Las Sombras were no doubt chasing him. Which meant they probably weren't too far behind. He was right about needing to get out of here. She just wasn't going to take him with her.

"So go."

He started hobbling toward her car.

"Where are you going?"

He stopped and turned. "To the car."

"What makes you think I'm going to let you in my car, *Nico*?"

"Alexis, we don't—"

"How do you know my name?" A chill raced up her spine. Her name coming from his mouth was familiar. "Who are you?" *Why* was he so familiar?

Breaking tree limbs sounded behind her. She spun around. They came from the direction he'd run from.

"I'm undercover and my identity was blown. They know I'm a cop. We can stand here and I can explain while they're getting closer or I can explain in the car. We have to move now." He stumbled a bit before regaining his balance.

She didn't hesitate to climb in the driver's door—and ignored the way he frowned at her favoring her bad leg as he climbed into the back seat.

Alexis had the SUV in Drive just as three men came bursting through the forest line. There was no time to figure out why this man seemed so familiar.

"Go," Nico yelled.

One of the men on the side of the road raised a gun.

She mashed the accelerator and the SUV roared forward. *I can't believe I'm helping one of them.*

A man jumped for the rear door handle, no doubt hoping to gain access. His hand slipped off the back door and he fell to the ground.

Alexis winced. *Lord.* She gasped a breath as the prayer faltered. How had her life come to this?

She glanced in the rearview mirror and saw one of the men aim at her vehicle. The other on the ground, unmoving.

"Get down," she yelled.

The back window shattered.

She steered the SUV around a curve in the road and could no longer see the men who'd shot at them. Nico groaned and sat up.

"I've got to get you to a hospital. You could have internal bleeding and that knife wound probably needs stitches." She split her attention between the road and watching him. She didn't exactly trust him.

If he really was a cop, he'd want to go to the hospital.

"No," he barked.

Of course. A *criminal* wouldn't want to go to a hospital.

She reached for her purse in the passenger seat and

blindly felt around for her cell phone. She wanted to have it close in case something happened.

"I'm sorry. I didn't mean to be so gruff. No hospital. I don't trust anyone. I just—" he laid his head back against the seat "—need you." His head flopped to the right as she turned onto the drive that would lead to the cabin.

"You need me to what?" She looked in the rearview mirror but Nico, or whatever his name was, was unconscious. His head had lolled to the side.

Now would be the time to take him to the hospital. He couldn't argue or stop her for that matter. But he said he didn't trust anyone. Trust wasn't something she gave easily anymore. Her trust had been broken and her husband had died as a result. She wouldn't be trusting the man in the back seat just yet, but he surely had the information she needed. He might know something about Tony's death, which meant he could help her in exchange for her helping him.

So, she would do as he asked. For now. What had gotten into her?

She'd been investigating her husband's death, and now she was sympathizing with the enemy. But he knew her name. And something about him said there was more below the surface.

She needed to know how he knew her name and what else he might know about Tony's death. If he really was undercover, she should help him.

Alexis parked as close as she could to the cabin door. She wasn't sure if Nico was just asleep or unconscious. She raced up the porch steps and unlocked the cabin before running back to the SUV. Nico was slumped over to the right.

She reached across and shook his shoulder. "Nico, we're here."

He didn't answer. Didn't even move. She tried again, a little more forcefully. Still nothing.

It was starting to snow. She needed to get him inside the house but how? Even if her body was at one hundred percent, she'd barely have been able to get him inside. But now, with her injury, she'd never be able to.

She grabbed his left arm, pulled him to a sitting position and gently turned his bearded face to her. She tapped him on the cheek.

"Nico. I need you to wake up."

His eyes opened. "Alexis," he groaned.

She had no idea who this man really was, but he knew her. Other than his voice, nothing about him was familiar. He could've been making up that entire thing about being undercover. She had no idea, but there would be time for that later. Right now, she needed to get him inside.

"Good. You're awake. Let's get you inside." She stepped back while Nico turned to get out. His feet hit the ground and instead of standing, he started to crumple.

She reached out and caught him. His body weight jerked her forward and the familiar twinge in her back roared to life. She ignored the pain and looped Nico's arm around her shoulder.

"Nico, I really need you to help." Pain radiated down her right leg. "Please." Her voice sounded wobbly to her own ears.

Nico must have understood the gravity of her plea and began to hold his own weight. Together they made it to the couch in the living room, where she guided him to lie down.

She needed to tend to his wounds but first the SUV needed to be moved and the missing back window covered. She pulled an afghan blanket off the back of the couch and covered him up. His eyes were closed and his breathing was even.

She turned to go and he grabbed her wrist. Panic bubbled in her chest. She'd been too trusting.

"Thank you," he murmured before closing his eyes and letting his head fall to the cushion.

"You're welcome." She pulled her arm free and limped to the front door.

If he really wanted to thank her, he could tell her everything she needed to know about Las Sombras.

Just as soon as he woke up.

Nick was aware of a fire crackling somewhere in the distance. He tried to force his eyes open, but they wouldn't cooperate. He was cold. So cold his teeth chattered. He tried to roll and curl up for heat, but his limbs were so heavy and all of his muscles ached. Where was he? Had Las Sombras caught up to him? He struggled to sit up.

"Nico." A female voice reached through the haze as a hand gently pushed him back to a lying position.

That voice. He knew it. He fought his heavy lids and peered at the oval face framed by dark hair. "Alexis?"

"You're safe now."

"Where are we?" Were Las Sombras closing in on them?

"We're at a secluded cabin. No one knows we're here. You need to relax and get some rest."

He'd made it to Tony's cabin. Relief washed over him.

"Are you okay?" He remembered the shattering of glass as she sped away from Las Sombras but he didn't remember anything after that.

"I'm fine. Here's something for the pain. Take it and get some rest." She held out a cup and some pills.

He took the pills and the cool water soothed his aching throat. His eyes closed and he let his head rest on the pillow. Alexis pulled the blanket up to cover him. As warmth enveloped him, the crackling fire lured him to sleep.

Nick's eyes flew open and he sat up straight. How long had he been unconscious? Light streamed from a window.

Every muscle in his body screamed in protest. A fire was dying in the fireplace across the room from him. Where was he? The escape from Las Sombras came crashing back. Alexis had saved his life.

He turned and set his feet on the floor, pulling the afghan off as he did. A draft immediately cooled his left leg. He looked down to see his pant leg was missing.

"I needed to dress the wound." Alexis walked out from what he assumed was the bedroom and stood in front of the fireplace facing him with her arms crossed. "I disinfected all the wounds I could see on your face and arms. I had to cut off the pant leg to get a better look at the knife wound because it was oozing blood. I didn't feel it was proper to do anything else that would require removing any more clothes. You've got a couple of stitches in your leg and the cut on your forehead has a butterfly stitch." She gestured to a bottle of water and a small white bottle of pills on the coffee table. "There's some pain medicine if you want it. The bathroom is over there." She pointed.

He'd escaped the compound with just the clothes on his back. The run through the woods had left him covered in tree sap and dirt. Not to mention the blood from the punches to his face and from the wound in his leg.

"I've set some clothes in the bathroom." She rubbed her hands up and down her thighs.

"Tony's?"

Her face darkened. "How did you know Tony? How do you know my name?" She cocked her head to the side and narrowed her eyes.

He wasn't surprised she didn't recognize him; they'd only met a couple of times. His appearance had changed after going undercover. Even he couldn't recognize himself. His face was gaunt and covered with a beard. His hair had grown longer. The swelling and bruises from yesterday's beating didn't help either.

He needed to tell her who he was but he wasn't sure how she would react. Would she be angry with him? She couldn't be any angrier with him than he was with himself. Tony's death was his fault. Her injury was his fault too.

"Answer me," she demanded.

"My name is Nick Anderson."

Her face paled and she dropped her arms to her side. "Nick?" She squinted at him.

He nodded.

A series of emotions flashed across her face before finally settling on anger.

"Where have you been? I confided in you. I told you we were intentionally run off the road and pushed down an embankment. I was severely injured and Tony died because of the accident. Did you bother to investigate? No, you disappeared. Leaving me alone. I thought they had gotten to you too."

He hadn't realized his disappearing act would affect her. "I got the call about the Las Sombras operation and had to jump."

"And the whole time you were undercover you never thought to call me and say 'By the way you were right. I know the accident wasn't an accident and I'm following a lead.'"

"You don't understand." He shook his head. "When I go undercover, Nick Anderson ceases to exist. I had to become Nico. I couldn't have any connections to my real life. Plus, I entered with the belief there might be a mole in the agency. And now I know there is. How else would Las Sombras discover my true identity?"

"That's good to know. Tony died and then you essentially died. I've been left alone to figure this whole thing out because no one believed me. Thanks to the roll down the mountain, they couldn't find any evidence supporting my claim. Tony bled out in front of me and I couldn't do anything."

Did she not realize how much he had believed her and what lengths he had gone to find proof? He was the reason Tony was dead. He may not have caused the accident but he'd been too slow to act. Tony said he'd noticed inconsistencies in reports and Las Sombras had slipped through their fingers too many times. He believed there was someone on the inside leaking information. It'd been almost a year since Tony came to him and subsequently died. Nick wanted those at fault to pay—and if he was the one who paid the price to make that happen, then so be it.

"You better get cleaned up. I'm going to go make you something to eat." She limped away. Another thing he was to blame for. He didn't have time to sit and dwell on Tony's death, her injuries or her accusations. He needed to get as far away from here as he could before he cost another friend her life.

Then she wouldn't be a target of Las Sombras like he was.

She wouldn't have any part in this.

She turned and disappeared into what he assumed was the kitchen.

He went into the bathroom, closed the door and picked up the clothes she provided on the sink. Her words tore at his heart as he stared down at the bundle in his hands. Tony wouldn't be using these clothes because he was dead. And Nick was to blame. Had he just been quicker to act on Tony's suspicions, she would never have been there yesterday.

After his shower, he removed the gauze from his leg and inspected the wound.

Alexis had stitched the wound closed and had applied waterproof bandaging. She'd done a great job. She would have made an excellent doctor had her world not been shattered and medical school put on hold.

He shook the thoughts from his head, finished towel drying his hair and exited the bathroom. He found his shoes and some socks in front of the fireplace in the front room. Once he was completely dressed, he made his way to the kitchen, where he found a plate with bacon, eggs and a couple of biscuits.

"I had some leftover biscuits and already cooked bacon. I've warmed them all up for you." She stood, hip leaned against the cabinet, arms crossed.

His stomach growled. "How long was I out?" He needed to develop a plan and try to see how much of a lead he had.

"We made it to the cabin at about seven thirty last night."

He looked at the time on the microwave. It was 8:44. Thirteen hours. He'd lost any lead he might have had. Urgency pushed him forward and he wrapped the breakfast in a paper towel. "I need you to take me to the bus station and then head out to your parents' place. They still live in the next county?"

"Why?"

"Because Las Sombras has seen your face. They're going to be looking for you to find me. Get out of town for a little while. Let me figure this out and get Las Sombras taken down. Right now, drugs are missing and they think I have them. They'll do anything, *kill anyone*, to get to me." A lead weight filled his torso. Would he ever stop causing her pain and grief?

"Let me help you."

He couldn't ask that of her. She'd put her life on the line who knew how many times already. It was his duty to see this through. Her life had already been upended because of him. "Thank you, but I need to do this alone."

She started to respond but stopped herself, shook her head and walked toward the door.

"I'll grab the keys and get the SUV started."

He followed behind her. "Let me. You need to get your purse and anything you might need while you're away. But make it quick." Time was of the essence. He just wasn't sure how much time they had left before Las Sombras found them.

She pulled a set of keys out of a bowl that was situated on a table near the front door. "And here's this." She pulled a 9 mm pistol from a holster on her hip. "It's loaded, with one in the chamber."

"No. You keep it." He wasn't going to take her only form of defense.

"It's okay. I have another in the bedroom."

The guilt that had started gnawing at him in the kitchen intensified threefold. He'd not spent a lot of time with Alexis but he knew from Tony that she didn't carry a weapon. And now she had at least two guns. Did she live in a constant state of fear now? He accepted the gun and tucked it into the waistband of the jeans.

"One more thing." She opened a closet door and pulled out a thick flannel and handed it to him. Another item of Tony's clothing she'd kept. His throat tightened as he accepted it with a nod. He turned to the door and was greeted with three locks, one chain and two dead bolts. This answered his question about her fear.

Once he was out on the porch, he surveyed the surroundings. Crisp white snow reflected the sun, almost blinding him. When his eyes adjusted, he could see that any ruts and footprints that they had made last night had filled in with a layer of snow.

"It fell last night."

"Beautiful."

The mountain cabin was isolated. The only sounds were a few tweets from birds hiding in the trees. He descended the steps and walked around the side of the cabin to where the SUV would be parked.

His steps ground to a halt as he saw several sets of fresh footprints emerging from the forest behind the cabin. Human prints.

Two sets led toward the right side of the house, and two sets to the SUV. The tires of the SUV were flat, no doubt having been slashed by the visitors. The hair on the back of his neck stood on end. He needed to get Alexis and get her out of here.

Las Sombras knew where they were.

Which way should he go? He could follow the footprints and surprise the men by the house, but it would only be a matter of time before the other two men caught up. It was four against one.

Something hard and cold pushed into the back of his head.

"If it isn't the traitor himself."

Nick recognized the voice of Matthias, the man who had given him a beating hours before.

"I want to end you. Right here. Right now. But you're wanted back at the compound."

Nick was sure it wasn't going to be a social call. More like an interrogation and then an example of what happens to a man who crosses Las Sombras. That's not what concerned him most at the moment. What would they do to Alexis? He shuddered at the thought.

"Check him for weapons," Matthias told the other man, someone Nick didn't recognize.

The man patted Nick down and relieved him of the gun Alexis had given him. Next, the man checked his boots for hidden weapons and when he stood, he landed a punch in

Nick's gut. The pain sent him to his knees, and the snow crunched around them as cold seeped into his pants.

Two more of the Las Sombras henchmen, Jorge and Raul, descended the front steps. Nick's gut clenched. He'd failed. Alexis was surely dead already.

"No sign of the woman," Jorge said.

The pressure in Nick's chest eased. She was still alive.

"She's here somewhere. Check the cabin again. Then search any outbuildings. Find her," Matthias barked.

The two men climbed the steps and reentered the cabin.

Alexis must have seen the men coming and hid. Hopefully, once they left the cabin, she'd make a run for it. It didn't matter if he lived or died. He just didn't want to bring her down with him.

Silence filled the forest. Goose bumps prickled his skin as a mixture of fear and the cold air settled over him.

Shouts from inside the cabin shattered the silence.

Nick's gut sank.

They'd found her.

THREE

Fear and adrenaline shook Alexis's body. Her hands trembled, and her breathing was erratic as she fought to engage the lock on the basement door. Cabins didn't usually have basements, but Tony had said the cabin had been built in Prohibition days when people had to hide the moonshine somewhere. She'd left the door wide open and waited for the two men who'd invaded her home to go in and investigate before slamming the door shut. Finally, the lock slid home.

She couldn't stand here and dwell. Not when Nick was outside with at least two more men. Plus, she wasn't sure how long this lock would last. She grabbed a kitchen chair and wedged it under the knob. That would help but the men had guns. The door and chair may stop them but they wouldn't stop bullets.

She left the men yelling and banging on the door and peered out the window. Nick was on his knees with one man aiming a gun at him while another watched the cabin. It wouldn't be long until one of them came to check on the cabin.

She needed to create a distraction, and she knew just what to do. She grabbed a belt and headed out back.

She pushed a snowmobile out of the shed, careful not to make too much noise. She aimed the vehicle in the direction that would drive by the men. She fired it up and used the belt to hold the throttle open. She released the brake and the snowmobile took off.

Multiple gunshots echoed through the mountain air.

She crept to the edge of the cabin, waiting for someone to come barreling around the corner.

"Alexis." Nick's booming voice startled her. "It's safe to come out." She held her weapon down by her side. Was it really safe or was it a trap?

She peeked around the corner. Nick stood with his gun aimed at one of the men. The other writhed on the ground, grasping his leg.

"How? They had you pinned down." She gestured to the two men.

"The snowmobile gave me the distraction I needed to gain the upper hand. Are you okay?" Nick asked.

"Yes." Her voice was barely above a whisper. She nodded to affirm her words and hobbled to him the best she could. Her pain meds were starting to wear off and the sciatica flared, sending pain down her leg.

Nick noticed her limp and grimaced. "Are you sure?"

She nodded and holstered her weapon. Was he disgusted?

"Do you have anything to tie him up with?" He gestured to the man lying in the snow.

"There's some rope in the shed. I'll be right back."

He looked between her and the man on the ground. He was trying to make a decision.

"I'll be fine. Keep an eye on him." She left and then brought the rope back and tied both men up, making sure the knots were tight and secure.

"How did you find me?" Nick asked the man.

A wicked grin spread across his face. "Las Sombras have people everywhere. We know everything."

Nick growled. "I don't have the drugs."

The man only laughed.

Nick turned to her, tucking the gun in the waistband of his pants. "They've slashed all the tires and I don't think that snowmobile is going to make it down the mountain."

He gestured to the machine that was now lying on its side next to a fallen tree. "Is there another way?"

"There's another one in the shed."

"Let's go," he said and nudged her toward their waiting escape. She led the way, opened the door and walked inside. She grabbed a helmet off the shelf and offered it and the key to Nick.

He accepted the helmet but waved away the keys. "You should drive. You're more familiar with the terrain."

She donned her own helmet, straddled the snowmobile and scooted as far forward as she could to give Nick enough room. Pain radiated down her right leg, causing tingling in her toes. She wasn't looking forward to the ride. It wasn't going to help the sciatica flare-up.

Nick mounted behind her and didn't sit too close, but she could still sense his presence behind her.

"Ready," he shouted over the hum of the motor.

With a squeeze of her hand, they were off. She followed her normal path down the mountain. Trees and brush were flying by. Normally on good days she'd take the path down and let nature soothe her weariness. But not today. Not only was it not a good day for her back injury, but it wasn't a pleasure ride. It was literally a matter of life and death.

Forty minutes later they broke through the trees at the bottom of the mountain and into the city park. She slowed the snowmobile and pulled it to a parking area designated for snowmobiles.

"This is as far as the snowmobile goes," she said over her shoulder. "They're not allowed to be running through town."

Nick dismounted and Alexis followed. The pain that had started radiating down her leg when she had mounted the snowmobile at the cabin had transformed into a burning sensation. She stood straight, putting weight on her injured leg, and her knee buckled. Strong arms wrapped around her, keeping her from hitting the cold ground.

"You okay?" Nick asked.

She nodded. "I will be in just a minute. My leg." She rested in his arms a moment, stretching her leg, allowing the burning to subside. It had been a long time since anyone had held her. She felt protected, safe. Like when Tony would hold her. Before he buried himself in his work and she'd come second in his life. But she wasn't safe. Not anymore. And she wasn't sure she could fully trust Nick. After all, he had disappeared after Tony's death.

She put her full weight on her leg and stepped out of Nick's embrace. Vulnerability immediately enveloped her.

"Thank you."

"Are you okay to walk?" Concern was etched on Nick's face.

"I am now." She looked around. "Now where?"

"Let's get to the bus station and we'll go from there."

She turned and walked toward their destination. Nick fell in step with her. Or actually in limp. They must look like quite the pair. Two injured people walking down an idyllic mountain town whose streets were lined with shops and restaurants.

Nick's head swiveled the entire time, keeping an eye out. No doubt for friends of the men on the mountain. He stopped abruptly, turned to face her and wrapped his arms around her waist.

"Quick. Hug me. Keep your face hidden."

Her heart beat a rapid staccato in her chest, but she did as he instructed. Hugging him, she turned her face into his neck, using the embrace to hide.

Nick tilted his head down and buried his face in her hair. "One of the Las Sombras guys is across the street. He just stepped out of that diner," he whispered into the top of her head. "I doubt he knows what you look like but I'll definitely be recognized."

"Okay. What do we do?" Did he have a plan? She doubted either one of them would be able to outrun anyone in a chase.

"Can you discreetly look across the street and see if he's still there? Brown coat. Black beanie."

Could she? Yes, she could. Did she want to? No, she didn't. Fear gripped her. *Don't let the fear control you. You control it.*

She must have hesitated too long because Nick loosened his grip on her and started to turn. She had to do this. She released his waist, stood on tiptoes and threw her arms around his neck, resting her head on his shoulder. She forced a huge smile like he'd just given her the best news.

Hopefully, the man was too far away to see it was a fake. But when she looked the man was gone. She scanned the sidewalk and saw a brown coat walking toward the park and the snowmobile parking area. Had word traveled that fast?

She dropped her arms and lowered herself back down to her flat feet. "He's gone."

Nick released his arms and stepped back. An icy chill replaced the warmth his body had provided and she shivered.

"Let's get to the station." He shoved his hands in the flannel pockets.

She heard what he didn't say. He was just doing his job. She was a means to an end to find the mole. Which was just fine. She wasn't about to become second fiddle in another man's life.

That was a close one—the bad guys and the hug. Las Sombras people were everywhere. Nick wasn't sure if Las Sombras had had the time to alert anyone of their escape down the mountain, but everyone in the cartel knew about the missing drugs and the role they thought he played in their disappearance. He was a wanted man, and that meant Nick needed to get them to the station and get Alexis a ticket on a bus to safety. Then he could figure out what to do about the missing drugs.

He had no business dragging her into this. But as much as he craved company from someone not affiliated with the cartel, he couldn't put her in any more danger. She was a breath of fresh air, even if she didn't fully trust him.

Could he really trust her though? She'd been sneaking around the compound. Despite the fact that he wanted to believe she wasn't working with Las Sombras, it was possible she was being used as a decoy. Someone he'd never suspect, sent in to trap him. He couldn't reconcile the woman Tony had talked about as someone who'd be involved with Las Sombras—especially when the cartel were the ones who'd caused his death. But he'd also never suspected there to be a mole in the DEA.

"What were you doing at the compound?" No reason to sugarcoat the question. He didn't have time to play games.

"Investigating Tony's death. No one else was going to do it." Her tone expressed her anger.

"Were you able to find anything?" If she really was trying to find Tony's killer and she wasn't on the Las Sombras payroll, then maybe she had information he could use.

But that doubt reared its head again. Someone had leaked information to Felipe—otherwise, they'd never have found out he was a cop.

"Not anything useful." She blew out a breath. "Do you know what Tony was working on when he died?"

"We were in the planning stages of an investigation. Did he tell you anything about it?" He didn't want to reveal too much information. He needed to know how much she knew about Las Sombras and their mountain compound.

She shook her head. "He never talked about work at

home. He told me he didn't want me to worry." She kicked a rock on the sidewalk.

"Did he tell you about suspecting a leak in the agency?"

She kicked a rock on the sidewalk. "That was the only time he talked about it. He didn't give me in-depth details. Just he had a gut feeling. I told him he needed to talk to you."

That's when Nick had failed. Tony had confided in him and he'd dropped the ball. Instead of taking Tony's concern about a mole seriously, Nick had been naive, trusting the people he worked with explicitly. He hadn't believed a coworker could be dirty. He'd failed his friend. Now, Tony was dead, drugs were missing and he was being blamed, and his cover may be blown.

They fell into silence.

He searched every face, looking for those he recognized and those that recognized him. He didn't know everyone in the organization since he worked the docks and cutting floor, but he was sure they had all seen his picture by now thanks to the invention of cell phones. He could only hope he'd notice the moment recognition dawned on them and he and Alexis would be forced to run again.

They walked in silence, side by side. His body ached and his leg was on fire but he couldn't stop. Not until he knew Alexis was safe. The closer they got to the bus station the more crowded it became.

As they neared the entrance, he reached out and grabbed Alexis's hand. He didn't want to lose her in the crowds.

"Stay with me."

He could feel her trembling. Was it fear or the cold mountain air? He'd have her on a bus soon. Riding away from the danger.

But why did that make him reluctant to let her go? She was in danger here, and he'd just have to get over the fact that losing someone who understood what he was doing—and why—had given him a gift he'd been sorely lacking during his time undercover.

He led the way to the wall of lockers and walked straight to number 203. He knelt down and started fiddling with his shoes. To passersby, he was just tying his shoelaces. In reality, he was retrieving a key.

He reached under the lockers and felt for the magnetic key holder. Panic seized him as his fingers came up empty. If Las Sombras knew he was undercover, then they'd know he had a go bag stashed somewhere. But he hadn't told anyone where he'd stashed it, not even his boss. And how could they have known this was where Nick kept his things?

This wasn't the drop location, the place he left the evidence about Las Sombras's illegal activities. He'd made sure to keep the two separate. He moved his hand a little to the right and made contact with what he'd been searching for. He pulled the box out, stood and slid the key out.

Inside the locker were a wallet, a gun and a cell phone for emergencies.

And right now certainly qualified.

Next to him, Alexis inhaled sharply.

Something hard jammed into his back.

A low voice said, "Don't move."

Nick froze. "What do you want?"

Alexis's left hand lowered. She was going for her gun.

He gave a small shake of his head. Her eyebrows furrowed, but she stopped.

He wanted to defuse the situation without causing a scene.

"Let the girl go."

Nick kept his hands where the man could see them and quickly assessed the situation. There was just the lone gunman. Were there any other Las Sombras nearby? If they weren't here now, they would be soon. Would he be able to get Alexis away in time?

"Not a chance." The gun was pressed harder into his back. "Now slowly hand over the gun. One false move and I'll have to shoot you and then your girl."

The man could see the gun in the locker but did he know about the one in Nick's waistband or the one Alexis had holstered under her shirt? Nick needed to act fast. Would he be able to do anything without getting Alexis hurt? One thing was for certain: he could not let them take her back to the compound.

Nick grabbed the gun from the locker and slowly held it over his shoulder to the man behind him.

"Now we're all going to go outside and climb into the car idling by the door. Don't make a scene. Got it?" To emphasize his point, he yanked Alexis closer to him.

Nick spun around. The gun that was once jammed in his back was now aimed at Alexis's side.

Nick held up his hands. "Okay." He knew Las Sombras. They wouldn't hesitate to hurt anyone, innocent bystander or not.

"Go." The man nodded toward the exit then wrapped his arm around Alexis, hiding the gun inside his open coat but keeping it aimed at her. To the crowd, it would look like a couple taking a walk. But Nick knew better.

He also knew that if they got into the waiting car, he was as good as dead and Alexis would eventually join him.

Once they were done with her.

FOUR

Alexis couldn't make her feet move. Her injury seemed to have left her hip scared stiff. Literally. Her mind screamed to walk, but her leg wouldn't do it. The gun was shoved deeper into her side.

"Walk," the man growled in her ear.

"Come on, man. Give her a break. She's scared," Nick ground out then turned to her. "It's okay. Let's go with him."

Was he out of his mind? She knew the statistics. Never let a kidnapper take you to a secondary location; that was as good as signing your own death certificate.

Nick bent down a little, catching her gaze. "Come on, Lex."

His use of the nickname Tony had for her startled her. No one had called her that since he died. Nick knew that Tony called her that. Nick had called her that once. Tony had growled at him, letting him know that no one could call her that, as it was his name for her.

Her mind went to Tony. A man who had trusted Nick with his life on a daily basis. But had he been wrong? She knew for sure she didn't want to go to the compound so she would have faith in Nick now. She nodded and started walking toward the exit. Nick *had* to have a plan.

She took shaky steps. Her injured leg was not cooperating as well as it normally would, the abuse she'd put it through in the last twenty-four hours becoming evident.

"Come on." The man with the gun practically dragged her to the exit.

"I can't. My leg." Before she could explain, Alexis fell to her knees in the doorway.

"I'll shoot you right here. Don't mess with me." The man started yanking her arm to pull her up.

"I'm trying." She got her balance, lifted up and elbowed the man in the diaphragm.

He doubled over and grunted.

Nick spun around and shoved the man backward. A shot filled the air; the man's gun discharged as he hit the ground. Ringing drowned out all surrounding sounds.

She could see Nick talking to her but she couldn't hear his words. She shook her head, not knowing what he wanted her to do.

Chaos broke out around them. People were running, shoving each other, trying to get to a safe place.

Nick grabbed her arm and pulled her up. He wrapped her arm around his shoulder and supported her weight as they ran out of the bus station. She didn't know where they were going but she tried as hard as she could, pushing through the pain.

They ran down the street and turned down an alley, following it until it intersected another street. They took random alleys until they were far from the bus station.

They were running again. They were supposed to be safe once they reached the bus station. But they weren't.

She was in over her head. She'd never thought about what would happen if she was caught by Las Sombras. She'd just wanted evidence to find Tony's killer.

Thank God for Nick being here with her. She might not have the best relationship with God—leaning on Him had been hard since Tony died—but she could still thank Him.

As her hearing started to return, she could hear sirens.

Nick untwined her arm from his neck and helped her sit down on a bench before sitting next to her. "Are you okay?" he asked between pants.

She nodded, struggling to catch her own breath.

"We can't stay here long. The police will be looking for us and so will Las Sombras."

"Why don't we just go to the police?" The police were the good guys. "They'll help us."

He shook his head.

"Why can't we trust the police?" Why did he think they were the enemy?

"Just trust me, please." He gently turned her away from the action.

"Trust you? I've been trusting you. But now the cartel is after us. We may not survive. We need backup."

"We can't call them right now, and not just because neither of us has a phone. Las Sombras have their hands in everything around here. We can't go back to the bus station and get you out of here. They'll be scouring the place looking for us. We need to find a safe place, and I need to call my handler."

"But I thought you said there was a mole?" He was contradicting himself. Was he telling her the truth or stringing her along? "How do you know you can trust your handler?"

Nick rubbed his hand down his face and winced as his fingers squeezed his bruised lip. "There is a mole. I'm basically on my own here but I can't let them know that I'm on to them. I left my wallet and cell phone back at the bus station. I won't be able to retrieve it. They know about the cabin so we can't go back there. We need to find a place to lay low until I can figure out what to do."

"I know a place." She didn't want to trust him, but right now he was her best lead to finding who killed Tony.

He looked at her. "I'm sorry you were dragged into this."

She couldn't say it was okay because it wasn't okay, but she couldn't blame him. He'd had no way of knowing she'd been sneaking onto Las Sombras property.

"It's not your fault."

"Where are we going?" He kept walking forward, following the sidewalk.

"There's a new housing development being built over on Spring Mountain Road. They've got a model house open to the public. We can go there." She pointed ahead. "It's not too far."

Which was a good thing, given how badly her leg hurt. And Nick wasn't faring much better than her. They both needed about twenty-four hours of sleep...and medical care.

"Won't there be an agent or someone watching the place?"

She looked at her watch and saw it wasn't even noon yet. As she blew out a breath, a fog mist appeared.

"Normally, but the house is closed today. I don't think there are any private showings scheduled for this afternoon. We can look at the calendar to confirm it. The front door has a keypad and I know the code."

"How?"

"I show the houses." It was a mundane activity meant to get her out of the cabin and her mind off Tony's death. It hadn't helped. "Since Tony died, I haven't just been trying to make sense of what happened to him. I dropped out of medical school because I can't keep up as a doctor with my injuries, and when I needed money I figured a real estate license was my best shot at a flexible enough schedule so I could keep working on finding the truth."

They walked the three blocks to the house, keeping to the side streets and shadows as much as possible.

Nick kept a vigilant eye on their surroundings, making sure they weren't being followed, she assumed.

They turned onto Spring Mountain Road.

"There it is." She pointed to the one-story modern house.

There were no cars parked in the driveway, which was a good sign. But just because the house was closed to the public today didn't mean that an agent didn't have a last-minute private showing.

She punched in the five-digit combination and the red light switched to green, allowing them access. Once inside, Nick turned the dead bolt. The main lock was a combination, but because it was supposed to be a replica house, the construction company had installed a dead bolt to make it exactly like those that were built in the housing development.

She led the way into the kitchen, where she sat down at the kitchen table. It was set as if waiting for a family of four to have a meal.

The kind of family she would never have now. She swallowed the lump in her throat. A family she thought she and Tony would have. But after two years of marriage, he started pulling away. Spending more and more time at the *office*. When she'd bring up expanding their family, it was never a good time. She knew he had an important job and he was saving lives but he was married to his job, not her. Then four years into their marriage he died. Her loose lips caused his death by telling the wrong person. Now she was a broken widow. She didn't deserve a happily-ever-after.

"I'm going to check it out." Nick walked around the house while she sat at the table massaging her lower back. Minutes later he came back.

"It's all clear." He lowered himself into a chair. "Is this set up like a real house? With water and phone lines?"

She nodded. "It has a phone. Someone sits here during open houses and answers the calls while greeting any visitors."

"Are there any showings scheduled?"

Alexis stood and looked at the calendar hanging on the refrigerator. "Nope."

"How'd you get this job?"

She gulped, grief clogging her throat at the memories.

"After Tony died, my friend Amy thought it would be good for me to get out of the cabin. She set it up for me to work the open houses. It gets me out once a week for a couple of hours and it's not physically demanding, allowing me the freedom to move around so my leg and back don't cramp up."

Speaking of cramping, her muscles were tight and the small circles she'd been rubbing in her lower back weren't working anymore. She stood up and made a fist, grinding it into her hip. She grimaced at the pain. Tight and painful now, loose and less painful later. At least she hoped it would help.

"Plus it allows me time to look into Tony's death."

Nick watched her. The more he studied her the more self-conscious she became. She dropped her hand. Getting some pain medication in her would help some. She knew exactly where to get it. Thanks to her weekly visits, she kept a bottle on hand. Nick could probably use some too.

"I've got some ibuprofen in the cabinet. Do you need some?"

He hesitated but eventually nodded. She grabbed the pills and two bottles of water and placed them on the table. She needed to excuse herself and do some exercises. A good stretch of her piriformis muscle would help with the sciatica that had started after last night's jarring.

"I need to do some stretches to help my back," she said and went to one of the bedrooms and closed the door.

He might be asking her a ton of questions, but it wasn't like he was forthcoming with details about his own life. He'd barely told her anything.

So why should she trust him? Plus, she was sure he was going to continue to insist she leave town. She had no intention of doing that. She wasn't going to let her injury stop her from finding who killed Tony. Nick would either help her or she would do it herself.

* * *

The pain etched across Alexis's face didn't help the guilt that had become Nick's constant companion since Tony's death. He hadn't been able to stop the attack that took Tony's life and caused irreparable damage to Alexis. And now he'd brought her more pain, emotionally and physically.

The interruption at the bus station meant he couldn't get Alexis to safety. Las Sombras would be watching it closely, waiting for them to return. What was he supposed to do? He couldn't save her now. He couldn't really save himself if he were being honest. There was a leak somewhere, Las Sombras knew he was in law enforcement and he didn't know who he could trust in the DEA.

On top of that, now thanks to missing drugs, Las Sombras had put a huge target on his back.

Because of all this danger and keeping Alexis safe, he couldn't drag her into it all. Otherwise, she would be targeted too—more than she already had been.

The cartel had to have access to DEA information somehow. Someone had to be feeding them intel. At least one of the local deputies had to be on the Las Sombras payroll as there had been too many close calls with shipments that worked in Las Sombras's favor to be a coincidence. He'd seen enough undercover to know they had to be greasing someone's palms.

That meant going to the local authorities was out of the question. Right now, he had nothing. Nowhere to go. No one to call. What he needed was evidence that would lead to the mole, whoever they were, and the cartel's missing drugs.

You have God. Tony's voice filtered in his memory. Tony had been a man of faith. Believing in a gracious God. Only Nick had never seen it. He'd only seen a God who'd let evil flourish. That wasn't a God he wanted—one who would let a good man like Tony die, leaving behind a widow. Even if

Nick wanted to know God, He surely wouldn't want him. Not when he was responsible for Tony's death.

His only option at the moment was to reach out to his handler, let him know what was happening and hope for the best. But he couldn't do that from here. The phone line could be traced and with the increased popularity of cell phones, pay phones were a thing of the past.

He knocked on the door where Alexis had gone. "Lex?"

He heard a muffled grunt. His pulse skyrocketed. "Alexis." He tried the doorknob. Locked. "Is everything okay?"

"I'm okay." He could hear the tension in her voice. Was she really okay?

He tried the knob again. He needed to see her for himself. "Can you let me in?"

"Just a minute." Her words were strained.

He was about to shoulder his way into the room when the door opened. A grimace contorted her face.

"Yes?"

"Are you sure you're okay?" He looked past her, surveying the room for intruders. "You sounded off. I heard something and you took a long time to answer." His survey of the room proved she was the only one there.

The corners of her mouth tipped slightly. "I was lying on the floor doing exercises for my hip and back. Trying to ease the pain. I'm not as spry as I used to be."

Her words were like a sucker punch to his gut. A reminder of his failure to Tony and the fact that Las Sombras had caused the accident that killed Tony and did this to Alexis.

She frowned when he didn't respond. "Is everything okay?"

He shook away the guilt. "Yes. I just wanted to let you know that I'm going to go try to find a phone to call my superior and update him."

"There's a phone here."

"I know but right now this is our safe spot. I don't want to take a chance on having my call traced."

"Let me come with you."

"No. I need you to stay here where it's safe."

Fear flashed in her eyes.

"I won't be gone long. I'll be back in no time. I just need to put some feelers out for the leak and see what I can find out about those missing drugs. Stay here and finish your stretches." He gave her shoulder a reassuring squeeze.

Nick slipped out of the house, making sure the door locked behind him.

He kept to the shadows as he made his way toward the heart of town. The irony in the action wasn't lost on him. Hiding in the shadows. From the Shadows, Las Sombras. Maybe he'd blended in a little too well during this undercover operation.

He limped on, trying to put some distance between where he made the call and where they were staying.

Nick walked into a hardware store and made his way to the paint section. He made a show of trying to decide on a color, grabbed a few blue sample cards and took them to the help desk.

"Excuse me?" He laid the cards out on the counter. "May I use the phone? My wife sent me down the mountain to buy paint and I left the sample card on the kitchen counter. Along with my phone apparently. It's a local number." He gave the clerk a sheepish grin.

She laughed. "Someone's in trouble." She lifted the phone and turned it for him to use.

"Not yet. You're saving me from going home empty-handed." He dialed the prearranged number and waited.

His handler picked up. "Blackstone."

"Hey, honey. Now don't get mad." Nick used his sweetest get-out-of-trouble voice.

"You've been compromised," Agent Shane Blackstone said.

"Yes. I left my phone and the color sample on the counter." Nick started rearranging the color cards in front of him.

"Where are you?" Agent Blackstone's voice was calm and collected. Nick imagined Blackstone's dark brows furrowing as he scrambled for a pen and paper to take notes.

"I made it to the hardware store but couldn't remember the name of the color you wanted." He tapped the card on the right.

"Are you safe? We're preparing to conduct a raid on a compound in New Mexico."

"Yes, I know I'm forgetful." He acted remorseful to sell the call.

"I can have someone there first thing in the morning." Blackstone's voice was gruff.

"Okay, great. That's the one I thought it was but wanted to make sure. I've still got to run to the post office."

"Post office. Got it. Tomorrow morning at eight." The line went dead.

"Love you too." He cradled the phone and pushed it back to the clerk. "Thank you. Now to get the paint and some supplies."

He went back to the paint section and looked around, waiting for an opportunity to sneak out. He wanted to get Alexis to safety so he could go back to work. Even though he hadn't found the person responsible for the accident that killed Tony, they were conducting a raid. Was his work undercover doing some good? Were they raiding one of the cartel's suppliers? Maybe this would start the cartel crumbling.

For now he and Alexis were safe, and no one knew where they were.

FIVE

Alexis paced the living room while massaging her hip. Nick had been gone thirty minutes. Was he hurt? Had he been captured? What was she supposed to do? He said no police. He was afraid even his unit was compromised. She wasn't even sure she could trust him. She had nowhere to go and no one to count on. She was alone.

Chin up, Lex. Tony's voice floated through her mind. *God's got this.*

Tony, always the faithful one. Even when he was lying in the car, life seeping out of him, he'd been so confident God was going to take care of them. Alexis had tried to cling to that faith after he died, but she wasn't strong enough. God had let her husband die and she was also left in unbearable pain, physically and emotionally. How was that taking care of them? A sob rose in her throat but she swallowed it down. Now was not the time to dwell on the past and pain.

She walked to the front door. She didn't know where she'd go but she couldn't stay here.

The door handle jiggled and the sound of buttons being pushed on the keypad lock made her retreat. Was it Nick or was it the men coming for her? If it was them, she wasn't going down without a fight.

She pulled the gun she'd holstered after Nick left and released the safety. Her hand trembled as her finger rested near the trigger.

Never keep your finger on the trigger. You don't want to accidentally pull it. Her gun instructor's instructions were permanently imprinted in her mind.

She ducked around the corner and waited. The door opened and cast natural light across the living area. She took deep steadying breaths, willing her heart to slow.

"Alexis. It's Nick."

The sound of his voice instantly calmed her. She reengaged the safety and holstered the gun.

The door shut behind him and he walked fully into the living room.

"My handler is sending someone to get us but it won't be until tomorrow morning."

Anxiety gnawed at her stomach. "Why so long?" She didn't like the idea of waiting that long. This place only offered them a facsimile of safety. Not the real thing.

"They're raiding a place as we speak. All available agents are assisting." He took a seat on the love seat.

"Oh. So, we just stay here until then?" She crossed her arms over her chest.

"Yes."

"Okay." She walked over to the oversize armchair positioned next to the love seat and sat down. "We just wait."

"I know it's not ideal but you said this place is closed today, right?"

She nodded.

"No one knows we're here. I made sure I wasn't followed. We'll be able to get some rest. It will do your injury some good, I'm sure."

What did he know about her injury? He'd seen her one time in the hospital and then disappeared. They slipped into an uncomfortable silence.

"Tell me more about why you were at the compound?" Nick's voice was loud in the quiet room.

His question surprised her. She'd already told him. "What do you mean?"

"Before I got clobbered, I saw you at the compound. What exactly were you doing there?" He eyed her.

"I was trying to find evidence to hand over to the police. Proof of their dealings."

"How'd you know about the compound?" He leaned forward and rested his forearms on his thighs, then winced and straightened when he hit his stitches.

"What are you getting at?" Was he accusing her of something?

"I'm just trying to put all the pieces together." He leaned back.

"I moved to the cabin after I was released from the hospital. I was packing up Tony's things and found some notes." She shrugged.

Nick sat up straight. "What kind of notes?"

"A map of the compound. Tony had marked spots around the compound. There were some random times and dates. After a few visits I figured out the marks were weak spots in the fence. I can only assume the dates and times had to do with drug deliveries."

"And you didn't take this to the authorities?"

"I couldn't. The DEA didn't believe the car accident was an intentional act to kill Tony. And all I have are just some drawings. That's why I was at the compound, trying to find more evidence to add to it."

"So, you'd been on the compound before yesterday?" He frowned.

"Not really." She fidgeted with the hem of her shirt. "I had been to all the weak spots and did surveillance and took notes. You know, how often did someone walk by, what time, etc. Yesterday was the first time I'd gone onto the property."

"Why yesterday?"

"I don't know. It was a spur-of-the-moment decision."

Had it been God? Had He sent her there to make sure Nick got free from Las Sombras?

"Do you have the notes with you?"

"I don't have my notes but I've stared at Tony's map so much I can draw it." She stood and went to the desk, pulled out a notepad and pen, and started drawing the map she'd seen too many times.

She handed the finished map to Nick. He stared at it. Brows furrowed.

"This is accurate. I mean the shape and positioning of the buildings. Of course, I didn't know about the weaknesses." He studied the drawing and rubbed his chin. "Had you been able to get anything incriminating on your stakeouts?"

She shook her head. "Not yet. Like I said, yesterday was the first day on the compound. I was taking it slow, making sure I stayed out of sight." Only, Nick had spotted her. "Obviously, I wasn't very good at that."

"Well, as far as I am aware, yesterday was the first time anyone saw you."

"That's comforting. The first time I go onto the property and I get caught," she huffed.

"Don't be so hard on yourself. You're not trained for this, like me and Tony are." He paused. "Were."

Silence filled the room again. Her stomach rumbled and Nick smiled. "We never got to eat."

She stood and walked into the kitchen. "I've got some food here. There were days I had to stay during lunch and I left snacks to eat when I took my medicine." She pulled out a couple microwaveable containers of soup and some peanut butter crackers. "Help yourself."

She popped the lid off the plastic soup bowl and stuck it in the microwave.

"What happened?"

She turned and tried to lean against the counter but her

back was tender so she stood up straighter. "What do you mean?"

"The day of the accident. What happened?"

"Did you read the reports?" She didn't want to relive that day again.

"I did but those aren't always accurate. Especially if there is a mole involved."

She sighed.

"I can imagine this is difficult for you, but maybe you can tell me something they didn't put in the reports." He reached over and laid a comforting hand on her shoulder.

She shrugged it off and took a deep breath. "We were on our way to dinner. Tony thought someone was following us. He kept watching the rearview mirror. We got to a super windy part of the mountain road and the car rammed into the back of our car. We almost ran off the road but Tony was able to keep control. There was a chase on the mountain road. I was dialing 911 when we were hit again. This time the car pushed us into the guardrail, which gave way and we rolled down the side of the mountain and slammed into a massive tree." Her eyes burned as the tears threatened to spill down her cheeks. "Tony had multiple broken bones and internal bleeding." She wrapped her arms around her torso.

Nick waited silently. He wasn't going to push her for more.

"I had managed to clutch the phone in my hand. I called for help. Tony died before help could get there." Her chest ached.

"And what about you?" Compassion filled his face.

"Herniated discs, nerve compression and permanent nerve damage." She started rubbing at the spot on her lower back. Her constant reminder that she lived and Tony died.

"I'm so sorry."

She shrugged. What could she say that she hadn't already said a million times already?

The microwave beeped and she turned to tend to her soup and pain shot from her back, making her leg buckle. She yelped as she braced herself on the counter.

Nick immediately closed the distance and steadied her. "You okay?"

Alexis took a deep breath. "I will be." Once the pain subsided and she could stand straight.

"Why don't you go lay down?"

She straightened and stepped out of his grasp. "I'm fine. I don't need to be babied."

He took a step back. "We both need rest."

Her shoulders slumped. She'd let her pain rule her temper. "You're probably right." She opened the microwave and grabbed her soup. "I'll just eat this and then go lay down." She gave him a weak smile, limped to the bedroom and shut the door behind her.

Alexis opened the bedroom door and walked out into the living area. She'd slept fitfully during the night. Nick was lying on the couch. He looked at her and smiled.

"Good morning. I was just about to wake you up."

She looked at the clock on the microwave. "It's only seven. I thought the meeting was at eight?"

"It is but I want to get there as soon as possible and see who all shows up." He took a deep breath. "I'm not sure we won't be walking into a trap."

"Then why go?"

"Las Sombras won't give up until their shipment is found. Right now they think I have it. I've gathered enough information to bring them down. I just need to make sure it's in the right hands. Meeting with this agent is a step in the right direction. If everything measures up, I need to get you out of here as quickly as possible."

He wiped his forehead. Alexis tilted her head and studied him. Other than the black-and-blue bruises, his face was pale. Dark circles laid shadows below his eyes. Did he sleep at all last night? He was injured and still fighting.

She dropped her gaze to the hardwood floor and wrung her hands. Fighting hard to find the mole *and* to keep her safe. It had been a long time since someone had fought for her. She looked at Nick again and heat bloomed in her chest. Her protector.

She blinked rapidly. Where had that come from? She didn't have time to entertain thoughts of attraction. Especially when she was responsible for getting the man she loved killed. What if she said the wrong thing to the wrong person again? She couldn't stand it if that happened again. No. Everyone would be better off if she just lived a life of solitude in the mountains. Not to mention, if she was alone she couldn't get her heart broken when the man she thought loved her became distant.

Alexis didn't need them getting off topic. "Didn't you say you thought there was a leak and you couldn't trust anyone? Why would I trust your colleague instead of staying with you?" She didn't want to go anywhere. She was safe here, where no one knew where they were.

"You're in danger no matter where you are. With me or without me. Maybe this isn't a setup, maybe my handler and whoever he's sending are on the up-and-up. We don't know for sure, but we have to try." He touched her shoulder. "I need you to be safe."

"If you don't trust them then I don't trust them. I'm safest with you."

Something akin to regret flashed across his face and then it was gone.

Still, Tony had trusted Nick so she would too. For now. But she didn't know anyone else connected with the agency.

"Tony would've killed me if I put you in danger."

Alexis's whole body flushed. He was getting rid of her… for *Tony*? Her husband was the reason she was here—because he'd taught her to take care of herself.

This was unbelievable. "Let's go and get this over with." Assuming whoever they were meeting were indeed good guys, maybe she was better off getting far away from Nick.

Nick led the way from the house to an alley between two buildings a couple of blocks from the post office. "I want to surveil the area. See if any Las Sombras show up." He looked up and down the street.

Alexis saw several people coming and going from the post office. They all seemed harmless. After a few minutes of silence, Nick pulled her back into the alley, tugging her farther from the street.

"Did you recognize someone?" Her gaze darted to the alley entrance. Had they seen him?

"My handler just showed up in a black sedan." He peeked around the corner.

"Isn't that what you wanted? Go see what he has to say." Even in the dim alley, she felt exposed. Fear crawled up her spine.

"It's not that simple," Nick mumbled.

"How is it not that simple? You called him and he showed up."

"Right. But it shouldn't have been him to come. Why was he so close to the area when he works out of an office eight hours from here?" Nick delved into thinking mode. Finally, he turned to face her. "I'm going to meet with him. I need you to stay right here."

Unease settled over her. "Are you sure you can trust your handler? We've both lost too much to be wrong about this.

Maybe we can wait and watch him or I can get closer and see if anything looks suspicious."

Nick shook his head. "No. You should stay here. He's my boss. I've worked with him for years."

Alexis wasn't sure if he was saying that to ease her fears or his own. "But you can't be sure he's not the mole."

Nick's jaw ticked. "That's why, if something happens, you need to turn around and get out of here. Get back to the house and call someone you trust to come to get you."

Panic welled in her chest. *Lord, don't let anything happen to Nick.*

"Stay here. I'm going to go out the other side of the alley and up the street so he won't see which way I've come from. You still have your weapon?"

"Yes." She prayed she didn't have to use it.

Nick placed a hand on her shoulder, knowing where her thoughts had gone. "Watch your surroundings. If something happens to me, keep yourself safe."

She propelled forward and wrapped her arms around him and squeezed tight. "Please be safe."

Nick hugged her back before disentangling himself from her. "I will."

She watched him walk down the alley. She wasn't sure what had made her hug him. It was something she'd have to work out later.

Right now, she needed to stay alert and plan an escape. Even while she prayed it didn't come to that.

Nick turned out of the alley heading to the post office. It made no sense why Blackstone would show up himself. He should be hundreds of miles away. Nick had given him enough info to start rounding up some of Las Sombras's clientele.

He didn't want to believe his mentor was really working for Las Sombras. That meant Blackstone had betrayed Tony as well.

Maybe even caused his death.

Nick walked four blocks up, taking an alley to the road the post office was on, and walked the two blocks back.

He watched his surroundings, looking for anyone hiding, snipers. His heart was beating so hard he was afraid it would burst through his chest. He wasn't ready to die. Especially here, leaving Alexis unprotected. Nick had already failed Tony. He didn't want to fail now. Not with Alexis in the mix.

He knew that if he died today, she wouldn't rest searching for the culprit. And it would get her killed—something he didn't want to happen.

Blackstone was sitting in his car animatedly talking on his phone.

They'd gone over this scenario multiple times in their plan as the handler and undercover agent. Blackstone would remain in the car and pretend to be having an argument on the phone. Nick would walk by once, go into the post office, count to twenty, exit the post office and head back the way he came. Only he'd climb into the car and Blackstone would pull away.

Nick never looked at Blackstone, and Blackstone wasn't supposed to look at him. Nick kept his body language and gait as normal as he could. It was hard with the stitches in his leg Alexis had given him.

Just another thing she had lost—her medical career. He couldn't let her lose anything else.

He followed the plan and deftly climbed into the waiting sedan. Blackstone hit the gas and they were off.

"Where have you been?" Blackstone barked.

"What do you mean where have I been? We agreed on this morning at eight." Nick had to tamp down the rising anger. "I'm here, aren't I?"

"We've had no contact from you in two months. You've missed the last two drops." Blackstone turned right, taking Nick away from Alexis.

"This mission was a bust. I'm pulling you out. We'll get back to headquarters and regroup," Blackstone said, frustration laced his voice.

"We can't leave yet. Alexis White is waiting for me to come to get her."

"Tony's widow?" The inflection in Blackstone's voice sent chill bumps down Nick's spine. Had he just made everything worse for her by saying her name? Alexis's question about trusting Blackstone floated through his mind. No, Blackstone was a good agent. Nick was just being paranoid.

"Yes. She helped me get away from Las Sombras. Twice. They've seen her so she's on their hit list. We've got to get her out of here."

Blackstone signaled and drove around the block.

"I haven't missed anything. I made those drops, providing two SD cards." Things just went from bad to worse. As if the blown cover, mole and missing drugs weren't enough. Now they had missing evidence. A lot of missing evidence. "You're telling me you got none of that?"

There really was a mole.

"Greg alerted me to the first missed drop." Blackstone glanced over at Nick. "I told him to hold tight. When he said you'd missed the second drop, I knew something was wrong."

"Yeah, something is wrong. Obviously, someone is intercepting the drops." Nick shook his head. "How?"

Nick just didn't know if Las Sombras was getting to the drops before the DEA, or if it was the mole getting them first. "But we have even bigger problems because Las Sombras had a shipment of drugs taken and they think I have them."

"Why would they think that?" Blackstone focused on the road.

"I don't know. Probably because they know, at least think they know, I'm law enforcement. They probably think I took it for evidence." He now had two things to worry about—the missing drugs and the missing SD cards. All that evidence? Gone.

"What about the other cards?" Nick had been able to drop two other cards before the two missing ones.

"We got two cards. Corrupted and no good to us. The only usable information we have are the lists you've been able to copy, and meeting dates."

"You're kidding me." Nick slammed his fist on the dash. "This can't be happening."

After Tony came to him with concerns about a mole in the agency and then his *accidental* death just days later, Nick had suspected there was someone on the inside working for Las Sombras. So he'd made sure he had duplicates of the information, but he hadn't expected all of his information to be taken or destroyed—not any more than he'd considered Blackstone would get nothing.

What was going on?

Before he did anything else, he needed to reach Alexis and get her out of town. As far away from Las Sombras as he could.

"Stop here." Nick pointed to the alley where he'd left her.

Blackstone stopped the car.

"Let me get Alexis to safety then I can salvage the mission by retrieving the duplicate SD cards and hopefully find the missing drugs."

Blackstone whipped his head toward Nick. "You have copies?"

The hair on the back of Nick's neck stood up. He wasn't so sure alerting Blackstone to copies was such a good idea—any more than telling Blackstone about Alexis being involved. He hated doubting a fellow agent, especially a senior agent. But Las Sombras had to get their information from somewhere.

He didn't answer, just jumped from the car and ran down the alley.

He didn't see her.

"Alexis. Let's go." His chest tightened. *Please be hiding.* "Alexis?"

Where was she? Had she been dragged away by a Las Sombras member, or did she leave willingly? Maybe she didn't trust him. Or she was involved somehow.

Alexis stepped out from behind a dumpster. Only she wasn't alone.

Jackson, a Las Sombras henchman, said, "Look who's here." He pressed a gun to her temple.

Nick was trapped. He couldn't save Alexis this time. Tony would never have let her get in a situation like this. He would have protected her with his life. He'd failed Tony and it cost him his life. Nick didn't want to fail him in death. He had to get Alexis out of here and to safety.

SIX

Squealing tires screamed from behind Nick. He spun around as Blackstone's car took off. Sold out by one of his own. Nick's heart beat in his throat.

"If it isn't Nico..." An evil smile spread across Jackson's face. "Felipe is looking for you. You've got a lot of explaining to do."

Nick was alone with Jackson, who was using Alexis as a shield. There was no way for Nick to get a shot off without hitting her.

"Let the girl go." Nick had to get Alexis away from Jackson.

"No. Felipe wants to talk to her too." Jackson pulled her closer to him.

"She's innocent. She doesn't know anything. Let her go and I'll come with you." Nick tried to reason with the man.

"She's far from innocent." Jackson looked down at her knowingly.

What did that mean? Was she connected to Las Sombras somehow?

Alexis shook her head. "He's right. I don't know anything," she pleaded with Jackson.

But was she telling the truth? He couldn't sit here and debate whether Alexis was an enemy or not. He needed to save her then they needed to have a long talk.

"I don't care. What Felipe wants, Felipe gets. Now let's go."

"Drug Enforcement Administration! Drop your weapon."

Blackstone stepped around the corner, aiming his gun at Jackson's head.

Jackson didn't falter. "We're coming for you, Nico. Nothing will stop us from getting what you took."

Blackstone inched closer. "Put the gun down."

Jackson shoved Alexis toward Nick and spun around, firing at Blackstone.

Nick caught Alexis and shoved her behind him, aimed his weapon and fired at Jackson. Both men landed on the ground. Nick kicked the gun away from Jackson and knelt down to feel for a pulse. There wasn't one.

His attention turned to Blackstone. He was conscious, but his hand covered a wound on his left shoulder as blood seeped through his fingers. Nick switched from defensive mode to life-saving mode as he started to shrug off his flannel. Blackstone was their only hope right now. No way would Nick let him die. Not on his watch.

"Hold on. I got you," Nick said, as Alexis watched him take off the flannel she'd given him and used it to put pressure on Agent Blackstone's wound. "We need to call for help. Do you have a phone?" Nick asked Blackstone.

Blackstone lifted his arm and reached for his pocket.

"I got it." Nick used a hand to push Blackstone back down. "Alexis, come hold this," he yelled.

She jumped right in, taking over holding pressure to the wound. Blackstone grimaced. Despite how she felt about him, and Blackstone's refusal to dig deeper into Tony's death, she wasn't going to let him die.

"I know it hurts, but I need to do it to keep you from losing too much blood." Her voice was soft and reassuring.

Nick searched through Blackstone's pockets, looking for something. What was he doing?

He pulled a phone from the pocket and started dialing.

"No." Blackstone grabbed the phone from Nick's hand. "We need to keep you off the grid. I'll call."

They listened as Blackstone called 911 and advised shots had been fired with two victims.

Blackstone ended the call. "The car is right around the corner. You two need to be gone before they get here." His voice was weak but adamant.

"We can't leave you here alone." Nick voiced Alexis's thoughts.

They needed to keep pressure on the wound until help could get there. Depending on the bullet's trajectory he could bleed out before help arrived.

Blackstone gritted his teeth as he pushed her hand away and grabbed the makeshift pressure bandage. "Don't trust anyone. Get out of here. This case depends on you." He sat up. "Take the phone with you. Get those SD cards. I'll keep both of your names out of this and call you when it's safe."

Sirens echoed in the distance. Could they really leave Blackstone here alone? What if more Las Sombras came back? They could kill him before help arrived.

"We need to stay," Alexis argued. Blackstone was here now; everything was going to be okay.

"No." Blackstone looked at Nick. "This mission has been compromised and we don't know who is involved. You're not safe until we figure it out." Blackstone then looked straight at her. "She's not safe."

A chill rolled over her body.

Blackstone shoved Nick away. "That's an order."

Nick took the phone, grabbed Alexis's hand and pulled her to the waiting car.

She shivered as they drove past the alley where she'd been attacked and Nick's boss was shot. He was still sitting on the ground, his arm holding Tony's flannel over his wound.

Alexis looked down at her bloody hands. Memories of

her bloody hands and Tony's life draining away in front of her crept into her mind.

"I need to wash my hands." Her heart beat frantically in her chest. She opened the glove box, looking for napkins or wet wipes.

"We will when we get somewhere safe," Nick said.

"No. Now." She turned around in her seat. There was a jacket lying in the back seat, and she pulled it onto her lap and started rubbing the blood from her hands. "It's not coming off." Tears slid down her cheeks.

Nick reached over and grabbed her hands. "You're going to be okay."

"You don't understand." She hiccupped. In her mind, the blood on her hands wasn't Blackstone's blood. It was Tony's. "He's dead and his blood is on my hands." She pulled her hands free and started rubbing at them again.

"What? Blackstone is alive. He's going to be fine." Nick's voice was strained.

"No. He's dead and I'm covered in his blood."

Nick pulled the car to the side of the road, turned and placed his hands over hers. "Look at me."

She hesitated but did what he said.

"Blackstone is going to be okay."

"Tony," she whimpered.

Recognition dawned across Nick's face. He pulled her into a tight hug. "It's okay, Alexis."

He held her as sobs racked her body.

"It wasn't your fault." He continued to whisper reassuring words.

But it was her fault. Tony was dead because of her. If she'd just kept his concerns about a mole to herself no one would have known. But she'd opened her mouth to the wrong person, Stella Ford, another DEA wife. Stella must have told her husband, Tek. He had to have been the mole

Tony was looking for. Only Tek found out first, arranged for Tony's death and provided evidence he couldn't have been the mole when she'd accused him.

"We've made progress. Blackstone is here and he knows there's a mole in the agency. We're one step closer to finding who is responsible for Tony's death." He continued to hold her.

Did Nick know about Tek Ford? Was he a possible suspect on Nick's list? She closed her eyes and took a deep breath before pulling away. "What do you know about Tek Ford?"

Nick studied her face. "Not a lot. Why?"

"Do you think he could be the mole?"

"What makes you think Tek is the mole?"

Telling him why she suspected Tek would also mean admitting to her role in Tony's death and she couldn't do that. "A gut feeling."

"Did Tony mention him in the days before his death?"

She shook her head. "I'd met him a time or two and he always seemed sketchy." It wasn't a lie. She couldn't put a finger on it but she was uncomfortable around him. Of course, she'd only been around him a handful of times.

"I don't know anything about him but we can look into him. Right now, everyone is a suspect. We've got to get somewhere and hide the car until the commotion dies down."

"We can pull the car in the garage at the show house."

Nick turned onto the street. There were no cars lining the street. Nick pulled into the driveway.

"I'll run in and open the garage." She punched in the lock code and looked around the house. She didn't know how she would explain her blood-stained hands if someone was there. Satisfied the house was empty, she raced to the garage to open the door.

Once the car was tucked safely in the garage, Alexis

excused herself to the bathroom. She washed her hands, watching the blood disappear down the drain. She tried to let the fear and anxiety be washed away with it. But when did that ever work? Not since Tony's death—that was for sure.

How had Nick remained so calm through all of the chaos? He'd not only kept her physically safe but he'd also been able to calm her down when memories threatened to consume her. It had to be his training. Stay calm under pressure.

She stared at her reflection. *I'm not strong enough. Not anymore.* A tear slipped down her face. *You can be. God will give you strength.* Again, Tony's voice prodded her to trusting the God he loved. Tony trusted God. He knew that no matter what happened God was in control and could use the situation, whether a good or bad one. He said a bad experience could lead to God just as easily as a good experience. Was God really here? In the midst of all of this? Was he working all things together for good?

"I hope so." She dried her hands and wiped her face before joining Nick in the kitchen. He stood at the sink, scrubbing his own hands.

Maybe he wasn't as calm as he let on.

He turned off the water and grabbed the hand towel hanging from the refrigerator before turning toward her. His eyes widened and he wrapped her in a tight hug.

"Are you okay?" he asked as he stroked her hair.

"Yes," she lied. She was physically okay, but her emotions threatened to choke her. She squeezed him back, drawing from his strength.

"Now what?" Alexis was pretty certain what happened this morning wasn't what Nick had planned.

"I have to go back to the Las Sombras compound."

Horror filled her. "Why would you go back there? Is this about the SD cards Blackstone had mentioned?"

"Because all the work I've done this last year has been

useless. Someone has intercepted everything I've gathered. Tony was right. There is a mole."

Her stomach tightened as her memories of Tony's last moments came flooding back. The car chasing them down the deserted mountain road. Tony taking a sharp curve. The loud crash behind, the car slamming through the guardrail. All she could hear were her own screams as the car tumbled down the mountain.

"Are you okay?" Nick placed his hand on her shoulder. His touch grounded her to the present.

She realized her breathing was panicky. No one had believed the accident was an intentional act. No one except Nick. Although he hadn't been completely convinced, he hadn't discounted her account of the events. But then he'd disappeared. "Yes. Just thinking." She took a deep breath.

"I'm sorry." He squeezed her shoulder.

She wasn't sure how to respond to his apology. Was it for their present situation or did he know where her thoughts had been?

She shrugged. "It's okay."

"No. It's not okay. I've dragged you into the middle of my mess. I'm failing Tony all over again."

Empathy filled her. "What do you mean?"

"Tony came to me with his concerns, and I brushed him off. I didn't want to believe him. We're supposed to be the good guys. He trusted me and I let him down. I was too slow to help and he paid the price."

After Tony confided in her that he thought there was a dirty agent, she'd encouraged him to talk to Nick, his partner. She was to blame. She'd let it slip to a fellow DEA wife and Tony was dead twenty-four hours later.

"Oh," Alexis squeaked.

"If I had acted, Tony would still be here, and you wouldn't be." He looked at her. "You know, injured and grieving."

She nodded her understanding. "What could you have done? You've been undercover since the accident. What, a year now? And you haven't found the mole." Her tone wasn't accusatory.

"I failed Tony. I could have made some noise. Drawn attention to myself and away from Tony. Who would care if I'd died? I wasn't married. I have no one to mourn me."

"We would have mourned. You were one of Tony's best friends." Her heart ached that he thought no one would care if he was dead.

A shrill beeping sounded from Nick's jean pockets. Nick pulled Blackstone's phone out and swiped the screen. His face fell. "This is *not* good."

"What?"

He turned the phone around so she could read it.

Agent down. BOLO Nicholas Anderson and Alexis White wanted for murder.

Below the text alert were two photos of her and Nick.

"No." She shook her head, disbelief filling her. "He said he'd keep our names out of this."

"Which means he didn't make it, and that he's dead. The police must've found his body. And somehow they knew we were with him. He could have been wearing a wire or some type of recording device." Nick's jaw tensed. "But if so, they'd know we weren't the ones who shot him."

"He was alive when we left. We didn't do anything. We've got to go to the police and tell them."

"We can't do that. They won't believe us."

He powered the phone off. "We need to leave. Now."

"Why? We're safe here."

"We were. But I've got Blackstone's phone. They're probably tracking it now and the car too."

Hopelessness settled on her. “Where are we going to go?” She was out of places to hide.

“We’ll have to worry about that later. We just need to get out of here.” He grabbed her hand and opened the front door.

“What about the car?”

“Probably has a GPS tracker on it. Everything stays here.” He stepped out onto the porch and looked up and down the street.

More running. She didn’t know how much more running she could do. Sirens screamed in the distance.

“They’re coming for us.” Nick pulled her down the walkway and away from the sirens.

If they were caught now, everything she’d been trying to do since Tony’s death would all be for nothing.

SEVEN

The situation had just gone from bad to worse. If Nick had any thought of seeking help from the local police or even the DEA, that possibility was gone now that he'd been branded a murderer. And he'd dragged Alexis with him.

They trod down alleyways, staying off the main roads and away from any passing cruisers.

The only way to clear their names would be to get those SD cards, find the drugs and unmask the mole. He held Alexis's hand tightly as they neared the park where they'd left the snowmobile. He hoped the cartel hadn't discovered it.

"What are we going to do now?" She started to slow and her breathing became ragged.

Nick ducked into an alley, pulling Alexis with him. He was pushing her too hard with her injury. The stab wound in his leg was starting to become unbearable, but he had to keep going. It was no longer just his life on the line. He needed to make sure he kept Alexis safe.

"I'm going to find you somewhere safe to stay and then go get those SD cards."

Alexis started shaking her head. "You are not leaving me alone. I'm coming with you."

"You can't. It's too dangerous."

"Don't tell me what I can or cannot do. This is just as much about me as it is you." She pulled her hand from his and put her balled fists on her hips.

"I know. I'm sorry I dragged you into this."

"You didn't drag me into anything. If you remember I

was caught snooping around." She used her right fist to massage her right hip again. "I was trying to find proof that Las Sombras killed Tony. It's been a year since he died and no one is doing anything."

Compassion filled him. "I was."

Pain was etched across her face. "I didn't know that. I thought I was alone."

"I disappeared undercover. I was trying to find the truth."

"But I didn't know that then." Alexis threw her arms in the air.

"Now you do. So let's just get you safe so I can go finish my job."

"You're in no shape to go traipsing back there," she said.

"You're not exactly perfect yourself," he spit out before he could stop himself.

Alexis's shoulders slumped. "I know that."

"That's not what I meant." Standing there staring at her, he thought she was perfect.

"I know what you meant. But the truth is you need another set of eyes and backup."

He had to admit she had a point. Going into the Las Sombras compound alone wasn't a good idea. They would still be outnumbered but the chances for success would increase if he had someone watching his back. However, he couldn't put her in more danger. He shook his head. "I don't think that's a good idea."

"It doesn't matter if it's a good idea or not. One way or another, I'm going to find the person that killed Tony. You can help with that or not."

Why was she determined to put herself in danger? He couldn't force her to go into hiding, and talking her into leaving the investigation to him would be impossible. He didn't want to take her with him but he also didn't want to let her out of his sight. There was no telling what kind of danger she would walk into. Keeping her with him was the best idea at the moment.

"Fine. Let's get out of here. We'll work out a plan once we're far away from here."

"Thank you." She turned and exited the alley.

"Don't thank me yet."

He followed behind. He would do his best to keep her as far away from the cartel as he could for as long as he could. Maybe she would see reason and agree to let him take over.

A sheriff's car turned onto the road ahead of them. Nick grabbed her hand and pulled her behind a parked car.

"Get down."

Nick hoped they'd been quick enough. Getting arrested would not help them clear their names. He turned and peeked over the edge of the car. The deputy drove slowly down the road, no doubt looking for them. He watched until the cruiser turned onto the next road.

"Let's go." He pulled Alexis up and they ran the rest of the way to the park. He kept watch for additional cruisers.

The park came into view, and the snowmobile was exactly where they left it.

As they got closer to the park, he saw coats and scarves tied to light poles. "What's that about?"

"It's the coat giveaway."

"The what?" If it was a giveaway, then chances are people would start milling about and they'd be seen.

She walked over and unzipped a coat, freeing it from the pole. "Every year the church collects new or slightly used coats to donate to the homeless shelter and community outreach center. Some are placed out here for those that don't want to go to the shelter for whatever reason. That way everyone has access to a coat."

She handed him the coat. "Put it on."

He put it on and zipped it up, immediately feeling warmer.

It was a perfect fit. "You need to get one too." He gestured to the surrounding poles.

"But I have one." She put her hands in her pockets.

"Right. One that you've been seen in. We need to alter our appearances as much as we can to stay under the radar."

"Oh. Good idea." She walked to a couple of poles before finding one that fit her. She shucked her coat and he tied it to a pole. "Check your pockets for gloves and a beanie."

Not only did he find a pair of thick gloves but also a couple of granola bars and a five-dollar bill. He showed her his findings.

"Yeah. Sometimes you get other goodies too." She pulled out her own snacks and money to show him and then stuffed them back in her pockets. She pulled her hair free from the braid, did some sort of twisty thing and put the beanie on over her hair. Only it looked like she had bangs peeking out from under the cap when she really didn't.

A new coat and a different hairstyle would definitely help disguise her. He wasn't as fortunate. He didn't have much to work with so he'd have to just keep his head down.

They made their way to the snowmobile, and he fired it up and they drove into the woods and toward the compound. The drive up the mountain and to the compound usually only took about twenty minutes but that was by car. They were climbing a mountain with a snowmobile. He'd estimate it would take them about thirty minutes by snowmobile.

Nick killed the snowmobile's engine a couple of hundred yards from the compound. "This is as far as we go with this. We don't want to make too much noise."

Sneaking onto the compound shouldn't be too hard. Having lived here for the last year, he knew Las Sombras's habits and routines. "We'll go through the woods here. We'll come out on the west side of the compound. The building where

I hid the SD cards is right on that line. I'll climb in through the window and get the cards while you stay hidden."

"No way. I'll go in with you and keep a lookout."

He wanted to argue with her but knew it was useless.

She cupped her hands in front of her mouth and huffed warm air into them.

It was cold out. The gloves weren't working too well. They needed to get this done and get somewhere warm. The adrenaline had kept him warm for a while but it would eventually die down. The sun was beginning to set and the temperature would drop even more soon.

Where could he and Alexis go now and be safe? Without evidence there was nowhere they could rest. He just hoped they could get the SD cards and end everything today.

They walked silently through the woods. The only sounds were the crack of branches breaking under the weight of winter's frost, and the crunch of snow beneath their feet. The forest began to thin out and the clearing leading into the compound would be right ahead. Shouts from a distance stopped Nick in his tracks.

"What is it?" Alexis stopped next to him.

"Stay right here." He gave her a steely glare.

She nodded.

He quietly made his way to the tree line, keeping himself hidden. Multiple armed Las Sombras were traipsing around the compound. Were they mobilizing for something? Probably a hunt for him and Alexis. He made his way back to where he'd left Alexis.

"They must be expecting me to come back. No one is usually back here but now there are people everywhere. We'll have to find another way."

"There's an old storm drain at the back of the fence line. You can't stand up in it but it's not so small that you have to crawl. There's a wire fence over the entrance but it's not secured at the bottom. It was one of the weak spots."

He ran over the compound map in his head, trying to determine the best route to take once they were inside. "We'll give it a try but they're on high alert. We may have to come back." He hoped not. He wanted to get in, get out and get as far away as possible.

He let Alexis lead him to the storm drain.

"Here we are." She stopped in front of a rather large metal tunnel. "It's not blocked here but they've got wiring on the other side. Where are we going to go once we're inside?"

He'd been thinking about it as they'd made their way through the forest. "I think the best way would be to stick to the fence along the perimeter until we get closer to the building. They let the shrubbery grow up around the fence. Keeps looky-loos from being nosy. It's winter so the shrubbery has died but it'll be enough to conceal our footprints. Follow me and stay close."

Alexis nodded.

He stooped and entered the tunnel. It was dark and smelled of dirt. Their feet sloshed through a little water; not enough to seep into his boots though. It grew darker the farther they went and then started to brighten as they neared the other side.

He slowed to a stop just before the exit. "We're going to go right and stick to the fence line. But first, let me check it out." He edged his way to the exit and peered through the fence. No one was in sight. He reached down and grabbed the fence. It didn't budge.

Alexis pushed past Nick and started kicking the fencing covering the exit. It had been loose yesterday. But no matter how hard she tried, it didn't move.

Nick gently grabbed her arms and pulled her back. "You're going to draw attention to us if you keep that up."

"Right." She took a couple of deep breaths and marched back the way they had come.

Nick followed behind her until they exited the tunnel. They walked in silence until they were a safe distance away from the compound. "It was open yesterday," she huffed.

"They must have discovered how you got in and fixed it."

"Now what do we do?" She glanced at Nick. His hands were shoved into his jeans pockets and his shoulders were scrunched.

"They're obviously waiting on us to make a move, so getting into the compound tonight is off the list. We need to find somewhere to keep warm until tomorrow. I don't suppose there are any more show houses?" The corner of Nick's mouth tipped up.

She shook her head. "That was the only one that I know about."

"I don't have a credit card to get a hotel room, and the cash we got from the coats won't be enough. Plus our faces are probably plastered all over the news by now."

Lead filled her stomach. Not only was she wanted by Las Sombras but she was also wanted by the police. For a crime she didn't commit. She searched her memory for somewhere they could stay.

"When I was researching the area before going undercover, I remember seeing an abandoned ski resort farther up the mountain." Nick straddled the snowmobile. "Hop on. We'll give that a try."

Alexis held on to Nick tightly as he maneuvered the snowmobile through the forest. Finally, the headlights illuminated an old run-down building as they pulled up the drive. A Mountainside Retreat sign hung haphazardly over the porch of the largest building. Faded white lettering stenciled on the building named it cafeteria and administrative offices. Small cabins were set in a semicircle behind the larger building. Each looked equally run-down. There were no lights coming from any of the buildings and the chimneys weren't emitting smoke, confirming the places were abandoned.

Nick maneuvered the snowmobile around the large building and parked behind the farthest cabin. "Best to keep hidden for now." He cut the engine.

Together they climbed the porch. The window in the door was broken.

"Looks like someone's used this before." Nick turned the knob and the door opened with a creak.

Alexis watched as Nick flipped a light switch just inside the door. Nothing happened. "I didn't think there'd be electricity, but it was worth a try." He stepped farther into the room and she followed behind.

It was dark but from what she could see, it was a simple cabin with a small living room that had a kitchenette lining the back wall. There were two doors on the right of the room. She assumed one would be the bedroom and the other a bathroom. Springs and cushion foam jutted out from rips on the couch. An old broken card table lay close by. Trash was littered all over the floor and a mixture of mildew and mold clouded her nose. She let out a breath, creating a cloud as she exhaled warm air into the cold of the cabin.

"Looks like it's been abandoned for a while." Nick walked over to a stone fireplace and bent to inspect it. He reached in and metal creaked. "At least the flue opens so that's a good thing. It doesn't mean the chimney isn't blocked though. There's only one way to find out. Let's get some firewood and start a fire."

The cold was beginning to seep through her coat. They trudged out of the cabin and into the woods. A small shed was positioned not far from the back of the cabin. Nick opened the door.

"This is great."

Alexis stepped up next to him and looked inside. Dry firewood was stacked to the right of the shed.

"Let's get some of this inside." Nick stepped forward and picked up some logs.

The sun had dipped behind the horizon and the light was waning. Nick's arms were full.

"I think this will be enough for now."

A twig snapped ahead of them. Alexis froze and held her breath, listening for more sounds. More snapping. Someone was out there. She grabbed Nick's arm and held her breath.

"Get behind me." Nick stepped forward, putting his body between her and whoever was coming their way.

She stared into the darkening forest, looking for someone. A black shape ambled toward them. A bear.

Nick froze beside her.

"Don't run," she instructed him.

Adrenaline coursed through her. She set down the logs she had and grabbed two large sticks and raised them above her head.

"Get out of here," she yelled as she waved the sticks.

"What are you doing? Are you seriously challenging that grizzly bear?"

"Not a grizzly bear," Alexis continued waving the sticks and yelling at the bear. "Argh. Get out of here. Go on, get."

The bear took a few steps forward.

She matched its progression. "Go on. Go home." Her voice grew louder and firmer.

The bear looked at Nick for a moment before turning and ambling off.

Alexis let her arms fall to her sides and released a loud sigh. "Let's get inside." She grabbed her logs and walked quickly back to the cabin. Her heart rate slowed to normal once she was in the cabin with the door shut and the bear on the other side.

Nick stopped and looked at her, amazement written all over his face.

"What?" Why was he staring at her like that?

"How'd you know it wasn't a grizzly bear?"

"Just something I learned watching the nature channel. Our bear had pointed ears and no shoulder hump. Two distinguishing features of the grizzly are rounded ears and a shoulder hump." She shrugged.

"Okay. Good to know." He deposited the firewood next to the fireplace. "Gather some of the paper lying around while I look for something to start the fire," Nick said as he started looking through the cabinets.

"Got it," Nick said as he stood up from a cabinet he was digging through and looked around the cabin. "One more thing."

Alexis watched as he removed the battery from the smoke alarm above the sink. "Let's hope this still has some juice." He took the papers from her and wadded them up in the fireplace, then took a clump of steel wool he'd found in the kitchen and placed it on top.

"You're going to start a fire with a kitchen scrubber and a battery?" Alexis wasn't holding out hope that this would be successful.

Nick pulled the steel wool apart and mixed it in with the paper scraps. Then he took the battery and held it up for her to see. "I'm going to try. If there's enough juice in this nine-volt battery it will send a current through the steel wool." He touched the two contacts of the battery to the steel wool. The wool pieces turned bright orange as it streaked through the pile like lightning in the sky.

"Don't inhale the smoke." He blew on the glowing mass.

Flames licked the paper, igniting the kindling. He added some smaller sticks before bigger ones.

"Wow."

"Sure beats rubbing two sticks together." He poked at the fire, arranging the kindling and sticks, then added a smaller log.

"Where'd you learn to do that?"

"I paid attention in science class." Nick pushed back on his haunches and watched the fire. "I don't want to make the fire too big. We don't want the smoke drawing attention to our location. Let's look around for some blankets to help keep warm."

"We can also move some of the furniture closer to the fire and box in the heat," she suggested.

"I like the way you think. You look for blankets and I'll move the furniture."

Nick pushed the couch frame closer to the fire, then used a couple of end tables on their sides to create a barrier in front of the fire. It would be a snug fit for the two of them but they'd be warm.

Alexis threw two blankets into the cubbyhole. "Look what I found." She waved a couple of cans of food at him. "I've got kidney beans and carrots to go with our snacks. What'll you have?"

"Ladies first." He gestured for the cubbyhole and moved one of the end tables like he was opening a car door.

Alexis smiled and stepped in. He followed and put the table back. He sat down next to her and wrapped a blanket around her before wrapping himself in the second blanket. She spread the sheet over their laps.

Alexis handed him the cans. "Which do you want?"

"I'm not picky." He eyed the cans. Truth be told, he wasn't

all that hungry but that didn't mean she wasn't. "I don't suppose you found a can opener for those, did you?"

"As a matter of fact, I did." She smiled brightly and pulled an old rusted can opener from her pocket.

He took it from her. "It's seen better days."

"Haven't we all," she muttered.

They sat shoulder to shoulder and stared at the fire.

"Thank you," she whispered. Her voice was soft and vulnerable.

"For what?"

"For believing me." She fidgeted.

"You're welcome." He placed his hand over hers to stop her fingers from peeling the paper on the can. A wave of heat raced up his arm despite the cold of her hands. He looked at her face. She was beautiful sitting by the fire. The oranges and yellows danced against her cheeks. Tony had been a blessed man.

Sourness settled in his stomach. Tony was dead because Nick didn't believe there was a mole. Not only had his disbelief lead to Tony's death, but also he'd caused Alexis great pain with it. Both emotionally and physically. The best way to make amends would be to find out who the mole was and at least set her free from that pain.

Her yawn interrupted his internal guilt march. "You should get some rest. It's been a long day." He pulled his hand free.

She nodded and then rested her head on his shoulder. "You should too."

A loud howl interrupted the peaceful night. Alexis jumped and clamped ahold of his hand. More howls answered the first.

"Relax. We're safe in here." He squeezed her hand. "I covered the broken window and shoved an old armchair in front of the door."

She gently squeezed his hand back. “Thanks.”

“Get some rest. I’ll keep watch.”

After a few minutes her breathing evened out and a soft snore escaped her mouth. Nick smiled. He could see them sitting in front of a fire, his arms wrapped around her. She’d laugh at something silly he’d said and he’d kiss the top of her head. That was something he could get used to. Cuddling up next to a fire with Alexis.

Except she was his late partner’s wife and would still be if it wasn’t for him. Plus he’d been burned in the past. It seemed women found dating a DEA agent enticing until he got sent undercover or on some dangerous assignment and suddenly they couldn’t handle the waiting and wondering. He’d given up on finding love after the third woman said his job was too much for her. Sure, Alexis knew all too well what being with him would entail. Long lonely nights. After being through it once, she wouldn’t want to go through it again. No. He needed to separate himself and not let his emotions get caught up with her. It was for the best. He’d find her somewhere safe to stay and then he’d bring down the Las Sombras.

He gently laid her aside so she was resting comfortably against the couch. He added a few more sticks to the fire to keep it going. He needed to make a plan. Otherwise, she was going to end up like Tony, and Nick would have to live with the death of someone he cared about all over again.

EIGHT

Light began to filter through the windows and illuminate the cabin. Alexis stirred next to him. He'd kept the fire stoked throughout the night.

"Good morning." She sat up and stretched her arms over her head. "How'd you sleep?"

"Like a baby," he lied. He didn't want her worrying about him. She had enough on her plate. The truth was he hadn't slept a wink. The pain in his leg had kept him awake when his thoughts didn't.

Her stomach growled. "Oh." She covered it with her hands. "I guess I was more tired than hungry last night."

Nick stood up, his leg burning as he did. Hopefully, an infection wasn't setting in. "Let's get you somewhere safe, then I can look for the mole."

"Not this again." She balled her fists. "We've already established that we can't trust anyone. The best place for me is with you. We can find the mole and then we'll both be safe."

"You don't understand. You're in this mess because of me. You aren't safe with me. If you want to be safe you have to get as far away from me as you can." Guilt continued to gnaw at him.

"This is not your fault." She stood toe-to-toe with him. Although she was a couple inches shorter than him, he could see the fierce determination in her eyes. She was turning out to be stubborn.

"It is my fault. I don't want to bring you down with me."

"Fine. Banish me from your presence but news flash—

I'm going to keep digging. I'll find my way back here again and again. I'm not going to rest until those murderers pay."

He didn't doubt what she said. If he couldn't keep her safe by sending her away, he had to keep her safe by keeping her with him. They were wasting daylight arguing. He needed to accept the inevitable. Sending her away wouldn't keep her safe. She really was safest by his side. His heart, not so much.

"Fine. Let's eat and get started."

Kidney beans and carrots weren't the gourmet breakfast foods he wanted but it would suffice for now. When they were done watching the compound, he'd make it a priority to find some proper nourishment.

After eating the sparse breakfast, they made the trek to the compound and found a spot where they were hidden but could still see the comings and goings.

"What exactly are we looking for? You've been undercover inside the compound for a year and didn't find anything about a mole. What are you expecting to find by watching from the outside?" Alexis leaned into him and whispered.

Her words were a stab to the gut. Someone else acknowledged his failures. He didn't know what he was looking for. It's not like the mole would fall into his lap. He knew he had missed something somewhere.

"I know but now I'm not inside. I'm now a loose end. Maybe urgency will make them sloppy. Plus, you're here now. A second set of eyes can help. And you might recognize someone I don't. I'm sure Tony had other friends in the agency."

Alexis stiffened next to him. He shouldn't have mentioned Tony. "I'm sorry."

"Don't be." Alexis jerked her attention to an approaching car.

They watched quietly as a man he recognized as a low-level Las Sombras member pulled up to the entrance and stopped. One of the henchmen stepped out of the guard shack and approached the car. Words were exchanged and the car continued on. A few more cars came and went. Maybe this was a waste of time. Could he reach out to someone in the agency? Maybe someone in a different jurisdiction could help.

A small black sedan headed down the road toward the guard shack. A blonde woman was behind the wheel. No one he recognized.

Alexis gasped and grabbed his arm in a death grip. "We need to leave. Now."

Alexis blinked rapidly. She couldn't believe her eyes.

"Do you recognize her?" Nick turned to face her.

She nodded. Alexis had been closer to the truth of Tony's death than she'd thought. She'd never expected Stella Ford to be involved with Las Sombras. The woman was too cheery and wholesome. Alexis had been played and Tony had died for it.

"Who is it?" Nick prodded.

"It's your mole." Alexis turned and walked back through the forest. Her chest ached from the betrayal. She clenched her teeth until her jaw hurt.

How could she have been so blind? She'd focused solely on Tek and never considered Stella. Stella was supposed to be her friend. A confidante. Someone who understood what it was like to be the wife of a DEA agent.

"I don't recognize her. Who is she?" Nick caught up to her.

"I'll explain everything back at the cabin." She couldn't talk to him right now. She was so angry at herself.

The anger morphed to grief by the time they made it back

to the cabin. Nick shut the cabin door behind them, grabbed the blanket and handed it to her.

She shook her head. "You need it."

"Alexis. Your teeth are chattering." He wrapped the blanket around her, gathering the ends in front of her.

She hadn't realized she was that cold. She'd been numb after seeing Stella. She didn't remember much about the ride back.

"Alexis?" Nick stooped a little to look her in the eye. "Talk to me."

She bit her bottom lip and gulped down the grief that clogged her throat.

"Who was that woman?"

She shook her head. "It's my fault."

"What? What's your fault?" Nick rubbed his hands up and down her arms. "Talk to me."

The concern in his eyes broke her. She couldn't tell him. He'd hate her once he knew. She shook her head. "I can't."

He pulled her into a tight hug. "Yes, you can. Whatever it is, we'll figure it out."

She pulled herself free from his embrace. She couldn't accept his comfort. She didn't deserve it.

"Alexis?"

All this time he'd wanted to take her somewhere safe and she refused. Once she told him everything, he would force her away.

"Come on, Lex."

The compassion in his eyes was more than she could take.

"It's all my fault, okay!" she yelled and turned away from him.

She couldn't stop the sobs. Grief and guilt swirled within her and escaped in the tears that streamed down her face.

Nick spun her around and held her tight. "Shh. It's okay. I got you."

She wasn't sure how long she stood there crying and listening to soothing words from Nick. She needed to pull herself together. This wasn't helping either of them. She took a couple of deep breaths and stepped out of Nick's arms. A sense of vulnerability replaced his warm embrace. She unwrapped the blanket from around her and handed it to Nick.

"Warm yourself up." She wiped her face while he stood still, watching her with eyes full of compassion.

"Better?" he asked.

She nodded.

"Good. Now tell me about the woman," Nick said.

Alexis took a deep breath. "She's Tek Ford's wife, Stella Ford."

"Are you sure?"

Alexis nodded. "Yes."

"So, Tek is the mole."

She shook her head.

"How do you know?"

Nausea roiled in her stomach. Now she'd have to admit her part in Tony's death. "He was investigated and cleared."

Nick cocked his head to the side. "And you know this because…?"

"Because I'm the reason they investigated him. I was convinced he caused the wreck and would not relent until they investigated it. I think Blackstone only investigated to placate me. Even after the investigation, I thoroughly believed he was the mole until I saw Stella at the compound."

"What made you believe Tek caused the accident?"

She took a deep breath. "Because I let it slip." She put her fist to her mouth, holding back a cry.

Nick reached out and put his hands on her shoulders. "Let what slip?"

"Tony had told me he was suspicious of someone in the agency working with Las Sombras, but he didn't know who it was. I told him he needed to talk to you about it. Compare notes. See if you noticed anything."

Anguish flashed in Nick's eyes but he remained still, waiting for her to continue.

"I had lunch with Stella the next day. I asked her if she'd noticed anything odd with Tek, or if he had mentioned anything out of the ordinary. Tony died the next day. Stella must have told Tek and he had Tony killed."

"Did you tell anyone at the DEA?" Nick asked.

"Yes. I kind of made a nuisance of myself until Blackstone finally gave in and opened an investigation into Tek Ford. The investigation determined Tek was clean and had no connection to Tony's death. If I'd kept my mouth closed, Tony might still be alive."

She squeezed her fists until her palms ached from her nails.

"Oh, Alexis." Nick pulled her close and squeezed her tight. "You are not responsible for Tony's death."

She pulled herself free. "I am. I said something and Tony died within twenty-four hours." Her voice shook. "Who else knew about his suspicions?"

"I did." Nick exhaled.

"Right, but you didn't kill him."

He didn't move. He just stood there, staring at her. "I may not have killed him but I didn't save him either."

NINE

Nick collapsed onto the couch frame they'd pushed to the fire and rested his head in his hands. *I could have saved him. I should have saved him. His death is on my hands.* He squeezed his eyes shut, fighting the emotions that were rising.

"You can't blame yourself." Alexis placed a hand on his shoulder. "You've been undercover for a year and only now discovered Stella Ford is working with Las Sombras. It would have been impossible for you to discover her in the time between Tony telling you about the mole, and his death."

She was trying to reassure him, but it was no use.

"I may not have found the mole but I could have watched his back. And yours. I could have insisted he lay low and let me do the digging." He dared to look at her.

The hate he expected to see was absent. He saw only compassion.

She squeezed his shoulder. "Sounds like we both have some guilt to let go of."

He nodded. "Yes, we do."

"What do we do now?" Alexis took a step back and wrapped her arms around her midsection.

"I don't know." He tugged at his hair as frustration crept up.

"We've got to do something. Surely there's someone in the DEA you can talk to. I doubt the whole agency is corrupt."

She was right. Who could he contact outside of the local office?

Where was his old friend Declan O'Neil now? They'd done the training academy together and had even been in the same office right after graduation. Then Declan moved across the country, though they'd kept in touch occasionally through email.

"I've got an idea but we'll need internet access."

"The library has computers we can use. We don't have to sign in with anyone. We can just walk in, type in my card number and get on."

"Let's go." He stood up and headed for the cabin door.

She didn't move. "Now I'm coming with you? Because a minute ago you wanted to wrap me in cotton wool and leave me somewhere 'safe.'"

Nick was going to regret that.

"Tell me I haven't pulled my weight," she said.

He couldn't.

"Tell me I haven't saved us, maybe as much as you have."

"It wouldn't be true."

She stared at him, then nodded.

"Come on. Let's go." He held the door open for her.

He decided to park the snowmobile a couple of hundred yards from the tree line by the park. "We'll walk the rest of the way. We don't want anyone to recognize the snowmobile and know we're in town."

He let her lead the way to the library. There were two people behind the information desk checking books out to patrons. No one looked up at them upon their entrance. That was good. The library was pretty busy. Kids were playing games and reading books in the children's section. Several of the computers were occupied. Mostly teenagers, more than likely playing on social media.

She sat in front of a computer and typed in her card

number before giving him access. "There you go. I'll keep a lookout."

He sat down and logged in to his email account and opened a new email. She turned to him, bent over like she was inspecting his website.

"The sheriff just walked in."

He cautioned a glance over his shoulder. Sure enough, the sheriff was standing at the circulation desk chatting with one of the workers.

Nick typed a short message.

I need help. My cover has been blown. I don't trust anyone local.

Alexis placed a hand on his shoulder. "He's walking around. We need to go."

He hit Send and logged out.

"Let's go." He grabbed her hand and pulled her down a row of books. "Is there another way out?"

She nodded and pulled him in the opposite direction from the sheriff. Toward the back hall. Doors lined the hallway, study rooms and a few meeting rooms. A few of them were occupied. People looked up as they raced by. Nick cast a quick glance over his shoulder. They weren't being followed.

Once they pushed through the side doors, they walked quickly, making it a couple of blocks before turning the corner and seeing a deputy walking up the street. Nick ducked into an alley, pulling her with him.

"Play along." He pushed her back against the wall and raised his arm, placing his hand on the wall by her head, effectively blocking her face from view. Then he leaned in close. "Act like we're flirting."

"Hey," the deputy barked. "What are you two doing here?"

This was the end of the road for them. His career and their lives were going to end right here in this alley. They were about to be arrested and charged with murder and no telling what else Stella Ford and Las Sombras pinned on them.

Alexis froze as Nick's body went rigid, her gaze riveted to his. What were they going to do? The last thing they wanted was a confrontation with the deputy. Their lives depended on them being able to get away from this without getting involved with law enforcement.

The deputy's radio crackled. "Suspects spotted at the library. All units be on the lookout."

They were still close to the library. Would the deputy suspect them?

"Move along," the deputy grunted before taking off for the library.

Nick dropped his arm and stepped back. She immediately missed his nearness. Then common sense kicked in. What was she thinking? He was a DEA agent married to his career. She couldn't let herself get attached.

"It's safe to say going back to the library to check for a response from Declan is out of the question. You said Stella was at the compound."

Alexis muttered, "I'm sure she has a computer."

Nick's eyebrows rose. "Do you know where she lives? Right now she's the only lead we have. Maybe we can snoop around and find something. Maybe talk to Tek and see what he has to say about all this."

The idea of facing Tek Ford made her sick to her stomach. She had staunchly believed he was the man who murdered her husband, but the DEA cleared him. He wasn't going to help them. What if he was aware of his wife's dealings?

"Are you sure that's safe? What if they're working together?"

"It's the best choice we have at the moment. We're both armed, and we'll be showing up unannounced. That will work to our advantage."

She didn't like it, but he was right. "They live about a mile away. Is that too far for you to walk?"

She wasn't sure how his wound was doing after stitching him up. He needed a real doctor to look at it and prescribe some antibiotics. The last thing he needed was an infection to set in. He'd been walking with a limp as it was.

"I'm good. What about you?"

"I'll be okay. Walking will help stretch the muscles and relieve some pain." She'd stopped counting the hours she was up in the middle of the night pacing the front room, praying for relief.

Half an hour later the house came into view.

"There it is." Alexis pointed to the two-story house with wraparound porch. It was nice. Not overly expensive. Definitely within the budget of a DEA agent. Obviously, Stella wasn't flaunting the money she was making with the cartel. Of course, if she was working with Las Sombras and her husband didn't know, she would hide the money somewhere.

"Maybe I should stay out of sight." Alexis bit her lip. "After all, I did kind of try to ruin his career."

"It's not the best option for sure but we're safest together. Let me do the talking. Keep alert and be ready for anything."

His words weren't comforting at all. She made sure her weapon was still at her waist.

"Let's go."

Nick's voice ripped her from her memories. They strode up the walkway leading to the porch. He rang the doorbell. The seconds that it took between the bell and the time someone answered dragged on.

The door opened.

"Yeah," Tek Ford said, glancing at Nick before his gaze settled on her. His face morphed from nice and welcoming to stone. "What do you want?" he spit.

"She's with me," Nick answered. "We have some questions about your wife, Stella."

Tek turned his angry gaze to Nick. "Why? Because Alexis trying to ruin my career wasn't enough for her? Why are you on my doorstep asking about my wife? There's a BOLO for murder out on the two of you. I'm going to call you in." He reached for his cell phone.

"Listen," Nick said as he held up a hand. "We didn't kill anyone. We know there's an agent on Las Sombras's payroll. I was undercover gathering intel, but my cover has been blown and now we're being framed."

"Sure, buddy. Are you having delusions of grandeur? You retired and dropped off the face of the earth after her husband died. And she accused me of killing him." Tek turned to her. "You ever wonder if maybe he was responsible." He jerked his head toward Nick.

Ice shot down her spine. Someone else was pointing a finger at Nick. And what was it he said about Nick retiring?

"What are you talking about? I haven't retired," Nick argued. "Blackstone sent me undercover into Las Sombras."

"No. You took Tony's death hard and retired. There were no DEA-sanctioned undercover ops into Las Sombras. You might want to turn your sights on Blackstone and leave me and my wife alone."

Tek started to shut the door but Nick reached out and stopped it from closing all the way.

"Blackstone is dead." Nick shoved at the door. "And we just saw your wife on the Las Sombras compound."

Tek opened the door wide. "I don't know who you saw

but it wasn't Stella. She's in Boulder caring for her elderly father. Blackstone—"

A crack ripped through the silent neighborhood. Tek's head jerked back and his body fell to the ground.

Alexis screamed.

Nick shoved her to the ground, covering her body with his.

TEN

Alexis's lungs burned as she struggled for air. Why couldn't she get a breath? No matter how hard she tried she couldn't inhale. She was going to die. She stared at the porch ceiling and begged her body to breathe.

"Alexis?" Nick's face swam into her line of sight. "Are you okay?"

She shook her head as she grabbed his arm with one hand and patted her front with her other. Could he save her?

"You're okay. Just calm down and relax. You've had the wind knocked out of you. You'll be okay in a minute."

He helped her sit up. Finally, her body responded and she gulped air.

"We need to get out of here." He started to stand.

"Shooter?" She could only say one word; sentences would have to come later.

"Sniper shot. If they had wanted us dead, they'd have already done it." He helped her to a standing position.

She turned to check on Tek but Nick stopped her.

"He's gone. You don't need to see it."

Her vision swam. Tek was dead.

Sirens pealed in the distance. He pulled her down the walkway and away from the house. Was the shooter still out there? Were they running straight into danger?

A police cruiser turned onto the street and slammed to a stop in front of them. Nick halted, dropped her hand and put his hands in the air. He glanced at her.

"Keep your hands in the air and do exactly as they say."

Alexis did as she was told. The cruiser door opened and

a deputy stepped out, training his weapon on them while using the car door as a shield. “Keep your hands in the air.”

Chaos ensued as more sirens announced the arrival of three more squad cars, each deputy mirroring the first.

“I am a federal agent. We are both carrying weapons.” Nick yelled the words loud and clear.

“Keep your hands where we can see them.” The deputy turned to another uniformed cop and said a few words before turning back to them. “Both of you, keep your hands in the air and drop to your knees.”

Alexis knelt down, keeping her arms straight. Pain radiated up and down her leg. Nick followed the deputy’s directions as well.

“Now lay on your stomach,” the deputy said. “Cross your ankles and spread your arms out.”

Alexis assumed the position she’d seen used on criminals on television. Nick lay so that he was facing her.

“Tell them you want a lawyer. Don’t say anything else.”

“Why?” Why would she need an attorney if she was innocent?

He must have seen the confusion on her face. “We’re going to need help figuring everything out. Asking for a lawyer will buy us time.”

“Stop talking,” a deputy barked as he eased toward them.

Within minutes they were disarmed, cuffed and sitting up on the pavement. “What’s your name?” a deputy asked.

“Alexis White,” she responded.

The deputy turned to Nick.

“DEA Special Agent Nick Anderson.”

“Yeah, I know who you are.” The deputy gave him a smug smile. “You’re wanted for the murder of a DEA agent. And now we caught you running away from a murder scene.”

“I want a lawyer,” Nick said.

The deputy blew out a breath, disappointment written all over his face.

Deputies milled about the area, cataloging the scene, talking to neighbors. Nick and Alexis were eventually loaded into a cruiser and taken to the station.

"You okay?" Nick asked her.

"Be quiet," the deputy barked from the front seat. He radioed in to let dispatch know they were heading to lockup.

Alexis leaned her head against the window as Nick watched out the front windshield. She wiggled her hands behind her. Handcuffed in the back seat of a police car was not somewhere she'd ever thought she'd be. It wasn't that comfortable.

Nick sat up straight, his gaze riveted to a car up the road, parked on the shoulder with its hood up.

Nick twisted in his seat and looked out the rear window as they passed the car. "We have trouble."

"What?" Alexis turned to see what Nick was talking about.

Another car on the shoulder slowly pulled onto the road behind them.

Nick grimaced. "Those are Las Sombras members and it's not a coincidence they're sitting there."

Her chest tightened. Would they really dare to attack a police car in broad daylight? Alexis gulped. If Las Sombras attacked, they were trapped. They couldn't get out and their hands were cuffed behind their backs. They were sitting ducks.

Nick leaned forward to look through the rearview mirror. He had seen that car at the compound several times. The men looking under the hood as they passed by were Las Sombras.

The car was still following them. They turned right and

the car followed. The hair on the back of Nick's neck stood up. Something wasn't right.

"I think we're being followed."

"I said no talking." The deputy looked in the rearview mirror. He made a left-hand turn and the car followed. Another right. The car kept up. They made it to a straightaway. The car behind them gained speed.

The deputy radioed in for backup as the speed of both vehicles crept higher. The deputy tried a few evasive maneuvers but it was no use.

"He's gaining on us," Nick said.

Alexis looked out the rear window and then back at the deputy. Panic etched her face.

"That's a Las Sombras guy. He's tailing us." Nick directed his next sentence to the deputy. "I wouldn't be surprised if he tries to force us off the road."

The deputy's gaze locked with Nick's. "What are they after?"

"Us. They know I'm a cop and they think I have their missing drugs. They're going to do anything they can to get me. Including pinning the murder of federal agents on me."

"He's gaining on us," Alexis said, bracing for impact.

The car made contact with the cruiser. Metal crunched and they swerved on the road. The deputy kept the car on the road despite Las Sombras's attempt to run them off the road.

The car raced toward them and made contact with the rear of their vehicle again. The impact shoved them forward.

"We're going to lose control," the deputy yelled.

The car left the road and began to roll down the embankment.

Alexis's screams drowned out the crunching of metal and breaking of glass. The cab of the car filled with dust from the airbag deployment. Nick's body was jerked around before the car finally came to a rest on the driver's side.

Fog crept into Nick's mind. He couldn't pass out. They needed to get out of there before Las Sombras came to finish the job.

"Hey," Nick addressed the officer. "We need to get out of here now."

"I can't." The deputy's voice was filled with agony. "My legs are pinned."

Nick turned himself and searched for the seat belt with his hands. Finally locating it, he clicked the button, freeing himself. Alexis's unconscious body hung in the car; her seat belt kept her from crashing down on him.

Nick leaned against the divider. "Give me the handcuff keys so I can help you."

"No," the deputy said. "Backup will be here any minute."

Frustration filled him. He knew the man was following protocol.

"We don't have that long." Nick looked out the front windshield and saw two men standing at the top of the embankment. It was only a matter of time before they came down. "Come on. We're as good as dead if you don't let me help."

The deputy tried to extract his legs from under the dash.

"The men in that car are on their way down here," Nick said. "What do you think they're going to do when they see we're still alive? They're not going to let us live. Now let me help."

The officer reluctantly produced the handcuff key and held it through the slats.

Nick turned his back to the officer and angled his hands to catch the keys. "Okay, drop it."

He caught the key and finally got his hands free. He tucked the cuffs into his waistband. Next, he released Alexis from her seat belt and gently laid her down. The back windshield had shattered, giving Nick an escape.

He stood up, hoisted himself onto the passenger's side of the car and opened the door. He could use it as cover but it wouldn't stay open because he was working against gravity. He could hear the men crashing down the hill as bullets ricocheted off the car. They were trying to shoot him.

Nick looked down at the deputy. "Give me your weapon and cuffs."

The deputy looked at him like he was crazy.

"Come on, they're shooting at us. Trust me." Nick gritted his teeth. "We'll all die if you don't."

Nick prayed the deputy would hand over the weapon and cuffs. The Las Sombras guys were armed.

Finally, the officer relented and pulled his service weapon from its holster and handed it over with the extra cuffs.

"Thank you." Nick took the items, climbed out and shimmied off the car. He cautioned a glance.

One man was just hitting the flat land. He turned to yell at whoever was left up by the road. Nick darted from his spot and hit the man on the back of the head with the butt of the gun, knocking him unconscious. Nick pulled the man to the back of the cruiser and cuffed him with one of the pairs of cuffs.

Grass crunched as the second man came down the embankment. Nick eased around the car. Mumbling came from the front of the cruiser. As he got closer he could hear better.

"Where'd he go?"

Nick cautioned a look around the car. The Las Sombras guy held a gun aimed at the deputy through the windshield.

"I don't know." The officer's voice was strong even through the windshield. He probably didn't want this guy to know he was trapped.

"Okay, there's no reason for you to live then."

Nick stepped around the hood of the cruiser and aimed the gun at the man. "Drop it."

The man looked from the deputy to Nick before slowly lowering his weapon.

"Place it on the ground and walk backward to the sound of my voice." Nick kept his gun aimed on the man. He hoped the man would cooperate and Nick wouldn't have to shoot him.

The man held his hands up as he walked backward.

"Stop. Lay on your stomach."

The man did as he was instructed. Nick used the second pair of cuffs and secured him. Nick shoved the man's gun into his own waistband and went back to the rear windshield, climbed into the cruiser and tried to rouse Alexis. She hadn't moved from the spot he'd laid her.

He patted her cheek. "Alexis?" She didn't react so he shook her shoulder. "Come on, Alexis. Wake up for me." Still nothing.

Her condition might be serious.

"Deputy, you doing okay up there?" Nick kept trying to wake Alexis.

"I can't move my legs," he gasped. "They're pinned under the dash."

Nick backed out of the car and looked at the embankment again. No additional Las Sombras men appeared.

He climbed on top of the car and opened the door, leaning the top half of his body inside again as he assessed the situation.

The deputy's legs were pinned, and it wasn't something Nick could help with. He needed a full fire and rescue squad with all their equipment. They were going to need the Jaws of Life to get him out. Nick prayed that the deputy's legs were just pinned and there were no broken bones.

Nick grabbed the mic that had fallen out of the deputy's reach. "What's your name?"

"Wheeler," he said through gritted teeth.

"What's your call sign?"

"C35."

Nick radioed in. "C35 to Dispatch."

"Go ahead," a voice responded.

"Deputy Wheeler's cruiser was forced off the road along Route 14. Deputy Wheeler is pinned under the dash and we have an unconscious female. There are also two Las Sombras in cuffs. We are in need of medical assistance and backup."

"Ten-four," the dispatcher continued. "Who am I speaking with?"

Nick ignored the question and handed the mic and service weapon to Deputy Wheeler. "I need to go watch for more threats."

Nick backed out and closed the door. He surveyed the area, watching for more Las Sombras. The area was clear. Sirens sounded in the distance. That was his sign to leave the area. He crawled back to Alexis. Still no response to stimuli. She definitely needed medical attention, but he couldn't stay.

She needed to be at a hospital.

The only way to save them both from prison was to get those SD cards.

"Deputy Wheeler, keep her safe."

"What?"

"She's innocent." Nick swallowed against the lump in his throat. "I'm going to get the proof. So it's up to you to keep her safe." He leaned over and pressed a kiss to her forehead. "Fight for me."

He backed out and disappeared into the forest.

Everything was black. Her eyelids were heavy. So heavy. Where was she?

Alexis finally coerced her eyes open and saw a tiled ceiling above her. A look to the right revealed medical equipment. Everything hurt, especially her head.

She reached to rub her temple but something kept her hand from moving very far. She looked down and discovered that she was handcuffed to a hospital bed. She looked around the room and found a deputy in a chair. He saw she was awake and immediately left the room without saying a word.

How had she ended up handcuffed to a hospital bed? She closed her eyes and tried to remember her last waking moments. A car crash. Everything came rushing back to her. Being arrested for murder and the police car being pushed off the road.

Nick! Where was he? Had he survived? *Please, Lord, let him be alive.* She didn't know if she could handle another death.

There was a knock on the door and a woman in a white coat walked in, followed by a nurse and the deputy that had been there when she woke up.

"Hello, Ms. White. I'm Dr. Adams. How are you feeling?"

"Like I was hit by a bus." The headache was just the beginning of the pains that plagued her body.

"Close. You were in a rollover accident. Other than some bumps and bruises and a concussion, you fared well." She did a quick exam, shining a light in Alexis's eyes. "You were unconscious for a little while, so I'm going to be keeping you overnight."

"What about Nick and the deputy? How are they?" She needed to know about Nick.

"I will let the deputy answer those questions. Do you have any questions about your medical treatment?"

She had some questions, but they weren't as important as finding out about Nick. " No, not now."

"Okay, I will leave you with the deputy. Just hit the call button if you need anything."

The doctor and the nurse slipped out of the room. Alexis turned her attention to the deputy. "Is Nick okay?"

"My supervisor will be here soon to ask you some questions." The deputy returned to the seat he'd occupied when she woke up.

"Okay. Can you tell me about Nick Anderson and the deputy that was driving? Are they okay?" Frustration was starting to build.

"No, ma'am."

"No, they aren't okay or no you can't tell me?" This man was frustrating.

"I can't tell you."

She leaned her head back and closed her eyes. A tear slid down her cheek. Things kept getting worse.

There was a knock on the door. The deputy stood and opened the door. A woman in scrubs came in holding a tray. She set it on the roll-away table.

"Dinner is served."

Despite everything going on, Alexis's stomach growled. She hadn't eaten much the last couple of days. She removed the tray topper with her free hand, revealing an oddly colored baked potato and some sort of meat with a light crust.

"Can I get you something, Deputy?" the woman asked her guard.

"Just a cup of coffee if you have one."

"I don't but I'll have the nurse bring you one." She smiled and flounced her hair, trying to flirt with the deputy.

"I appreciate it."

"You're welcome." She left the room and the deputy shut the door behind her.

Alexis ate her food in silence. It was bland, but she could

be grateful for the meal, even if she'd rather eat canned beans. With Nick.

There was another knock on the door.

The deputy opened the door. "Good evening, sir."

This time a man in khakis and a polo entered holding a cup of coffee. A badge hung on his belt, next to a holstered gun. The two exchanged words she couldn't hear and the deputy accepted the coffee and left.

The plainclothes officer stepped fully into the room and shut the door. "Ms. White, I'm Detective Longley. Before I start asking you questions, I need to tell you something."

She braced herself for devastating news. Instead, he started reading her rights.

"Now you're here in police custody because we found you running away from the scene of a murder, and you're wanted concerning the death of Agent Shane Blackstone."

"But we didn't do it." How could she convince him she was telling the truth?

"Okay. Tell me what happened." The detective pulled a notepad from his pocket.

"First I want to know about Nick."

"That would be Nick Anderson, the man who was arrested with you? He was not there when deputies arrived at the crash scene."

She let her head fall back onto the pillow and released a hard sigh. Heaviness settled on her. He had left her. She had to face the police alone.

Maybe he really was responsible for Tony's death. Leaving her with the police would get her out of his hair. He'd be free to continue on with whatever his plan was.

"Now, can you tell me what happened?" The man's voice interrupted her thoughts.

She remembered then that one of the last things Nick had told her was to ask for a lawyer.

What was she supposed to do, trust Nick had a plan and follow his instruction? But were his instructions just a ploy to keep her in custody longer? She wanted everything to be out in the open. Maybe they would believe her.

Alexis told the man everything from the beginning when Tony died up until the crash this afternoon.

The detective did not interrupt or ask questions. He just listened and jotted notes.

"So, you think that your husband was murdered but the DEA did an investigation and didn't find any evidence?" Incredulity filled the man's voice.

"I don't think he was murdered. I know he was murdered. And no, the DEA doesn't believe me. Their *investigation* turned up nothing. Nick believed me though." She tried to remain civil. She was back in a situation where no one believed her.

"How well do you know this Nick Anderson?"

How well did she know him? She knew that he and Tony were partners and friends outside of the agency. Tony had always spoken very highly of him. Nick had risked his life to keep her safe, but she really didn't know him that well. She didn't know if he was honest, or jaded, or if he had an ulterior motive.

She'd been trusting her life to a practical stranger. But she knew that Tony trusted him, so she had trusted him too.

Now she wondered if Tony's trust had been broken when Nick killed him.

She could sit in this hospital bed and go down a rabbit hole of why she should trust him *and* why she shouldn't trust him. But it wouldn't do any good.

"Any idea where he would go?" The detective asked a different question.

She had a hunch he was probably back at the cabin but

she wasn't going to spill the beans. She hadn't told him the exact location of the cabin and he hadn't asked. Yet.

This whole ordeal was a giant mess and she didn't know who to trust. Nick had left her to face this alone. Nick didn't trust anyone in the local police department and she didn't trust anybody in the DEA except Nick. But it was beginning to look like she'd misplaced her trust again.

She would keep that information to herself. "No, I don't."

The detective pinned her with an accusatory stare. "Are you sure? Where have you two been the last forty-eight hours?"

"Trying not to get killed," she scoffed.

He gave her a dubious look. "We've watched the surveillance tapes from the bus stop. We know what happened. What we can't figure out is why not go straight to the police?"

She remained silent.

"Look, you're a smart woman. Let us do our jobs. Give us Mr. Anderson's whereabouts so we can bring him in safely before he gets hurt."

Alexis was on her own. "I want a lawyer."

Relief flooded her. A lawyer would fight for her, and she could get solid advice.

But was she really putting her trust in the right person?

She knew she should be trusting God above all things, but He had seemed distant since the accident. She had been working on trusting herself, and now trusting Nick, when she should be trusting God. Maybe Tony was right. Maybe God could orchestrate something good from the chaos her life had become. She just needed to trust Him.

The detective's nostrils flared. "It'll be tomorrow before we can get a lawyer in for you. The deputy will be stationed by the door all night. Just let him know if you change your mind and want to talk."

He shut the door.

What was she supposed to do now? She'd started this journey looking for the person responsible for killing her husband. She'd had no idea it would drag her this deep into their world. She couldn't trust anyone. She shouldn't trust Nick, but the truth was that she did.

Had trusting him made everything worse?

Her stomach was full, and sleep called to her. Alexis rolled to her side and closed her eyes. Before she could fall asleep she heard the door creak as it opened. She rolled over to see who it was and came face-to-face with Stella Ford.

"What are you doing here?" Alexis frowned. "How did you get past the deputy?"

"Oh, the deputy will be sleeping for a while." Stella pulled something from her pocket. "Don't think about yelling. There's an emergency two doors down so everyone's busy trying to resuscitate a patient. You're all mine. And now I'll finish what I started on that mountain road a year ago."

Stella was responsible for Tony's death and was here to kill her. The beeping on the monitor increased as Alexis's heart rate spiked. She reached for the emergency nurse button, but Stella was too fast. A punch to the face sent Alexis's head swirling.

The pillow was yanked from behind her and placed over her head. Having one hand cuffed to the bed made it difficult for her to fight.

Stella was stronger than Alexis gave her credit for. Alexis fought the best she could but all she had was hot air in her face.

Her lungs screamed for fresh air.

She was going to die.

ELEVEN

What was he thinking coming to the hospital? This was the last place he should be, but he needed to know Alexis was okay. He took the stairs and checked every floor, looking for signs Alexis was there. He opened the door on the third floor and spotted a uniformed deputy slumped forward, asleep in a chair outside a hospital room. That had to be where Alexis was.

What kind of law enforcement officers were they hiring nowadays? Nick paused, then realized that the guy had been drugged.

Nick walked quickly to the room and tried to shake the deputy awake, but he was out cold. There was a commotion inside the room. Nick opened the door and found a nurse holding a pillow over Alexis's head.

"Stop," he shouted.

The nurse turned and he recognized her as the woman Alexis had called Stella—Tek's wife. Had she killed her husband in front of them?

She grabbed the food tray off the rolling table and charged at him. She swung the tray and he dodged it, leaving the door wide open.

Stella raced out. He wanted to go after her, but Alexis was hurt.

Nick ran to Alexis's bedside and pulled the pillow away. *Please, God.* Alexis gasped for air. Her eyes were wild until they landed on him.

"You're here," she said between gasps. "Thank God."

"I had to know how you were doing."

Had God put the desire to confirm her safety in him knowing Stella would be here? Whatever it was that led him here, it had saved her life.

Now he had to stop Stella from getting away. He raced out to the hallway and again tried to wake the deputy but it was no use.

Nick felt for a pulse. It beat strong and steady. He didn't want to alert anyone about the deputy until they were gone. He searched the deputy for a handcuff key, then went back into Alexis's room and shut the door.

"We need to get you out of here."

"I agree." She threw the covers off her body.

He looked around the room for some clothes for her to change into but her personal effects were not there. "We will have to find you some clothes."

He watched as Alexis pulled the IV from her hand and held pressure with part of the sheet.

"They usually have a supply room with a couple of changes of scrubs just in case there's an incident. We can find some there."

He grabbed her hand and pulled her to the door, then peeked up and down the hallway to make sure no one was watching. He let her lead the way to the supply closet. She went in while he stood out in the hallway keeping watch.

A few minutes later she emerged in a set of scrubs and plastic-looking clogs. It wouldn't be enough to keep her warm for long but it would be enough to get them out of here.

They sneaked into the stairwell and took the stairs all the way down to the ground floor. He needed to get the deputy some help. He may be just knocked out with some sleeping powder or it may be more serious.

Nick pulled the phone he'd found in the Las Sombras car from his pocket, powered it on and dialed 911. They needed to know about their deputy. Once the call was finished, he dropped the phone in a nearby trash can. He'd used it earlier to check his email to see if Declan had responded. They were scheduled to meet tomorrow afternoon at the park. But for now, Nick needed to get Alexis away from the hospital.

He took his coat off and wrapped it around Alexis. "Let's go get you somewhere warm." He led her to the car Las Sombras had used to push the police cruiser off the road. He'd been able to take it before the authorities arrived.

The ride to the cabin was a long one. Nick helped Alexis into the cabin and led her to the makeshift bed they'd made the night before. He insisted she keep his coat and he covered her up once she was lying comfortably.

"Why did you leave me?" Alexis looked at him with fear in her eyes.

"Because you were unconscious and you needed medical attention. I couldn't give you that. I couldn't stick around either. If we were both in police custody, then who was going to figure out the mastermind behind all of this?"

What he didn't tell her was that leaving her behind was one of the hardest decisions he'd ever had to make.

She stared up at him with those wide eyes he wanted to get lost in. "Why did you come back?"

"I had to know how you were." He wasn't going to admit to her that he cared for her. He was having a hard time admitting it to himself. She was his partner's widow.

"It's a good thing you came when you did." Alexis shivered. Whether it was from the memory of the attack or from the cold, Nick wasn't sure.

"Did Stella say anything before she attacked you?"

She nodded. Tears pooled in her eyes. "She killed Tony. And she was going to kill me. I can remember the look of pure evil in her eyes."

He sat down next to her head, reached out and tenderly moved a tendril of her hair.

"Were you able to find anything out while I was in the hospital?" She turned her face to look up at him.

The fire danced in the reflection of her eyes. He'd been so scared when he thought he lost her. He couldn't lose her. Not just because he felt responsible for her predicament and was duty bound to protect her, but also because she was beginning to affect him on a different level. He shook his head in response to the question.

"How do you feel?"

"Better now that you're here." She closed her eyes. "Safer."

Could she possibly feel the same way, or was his presence just about safety?

"What do we do now?"

"Declan will meet us at the park tomorrow afternoon. Tomorrow morning, we'll go over what we know so far. But first, you need to sleep."

Her face softened. "I want to hear your voice."

Nick felt a smile tug his lips. "Tony believed there was a mole in the agency. He tells you and me, and then your car is forced off the road, killing Tony. The DEA believes it was nothing but an accident but investigates Tek Ford anyway because you brought it to their attention. He is cleared."

Nick took a breath. "I was sent on an undercover assignment that may not even have been real. The only person that I can ask about the assignment is dead and we're wanted for his murder. We find Stella Ford on the Las Sombras compound, which confirms she is tied to both the cartel and possibly Tony's death. We try to talk to her husband but he's shot—"

Alexis flinched.

"And we're ambushed. I think the only thing we can do

is to get back on the compound and find those SD cards. It may not be enough to find out who the mole is, but it's enough to clear our names. We can just work from there."

Alexis's eyes had drifted closed and her breathing had evened out. She needed rest. Actually, what she really needed was to be far from here. Far from the danger. He was going to do everything in his power make sure she survived this.

Nick had been dutiful during the night, following concussion protocol. He'd woken her every hour to make sure she was okay. Sun had dawned and she'd found him sleeping. He must have been totally worn-out. He'd been going nonstop since he'd saved her on the compound.

She looked at his sleeping form. The bruising that marred his face had changed from blacks and blues to browns and greens. A sign they were healing. The cuts to his face had scabbed over. A brown beard speckled with red covered the lower half of his face, accentuating his strong jaw line. Brown hair fell across his forehead. Her fingers ached to move it away.

He'd saved her. Again. Everything she'd thought about him in the hospital had been wrong. He hadn't left her to face everything alone. He'd come back for her.

She pressed her fingers to her lips and found she was smiling.

He stirred and his eyes opened. He focused on her and gave a small smile. "Good morning."

Her face warmed. She could get used to hearing him wishing her a good morning every day. An ache quickly replaced the feelings. She couldn't let herself fall for him. It would end up just like her marriage to Tony. He'd love her for a little while, then she'd be brushed aside while he focused on his job. Leaving her alone.

"How are you feeling?" Nick stood and stretched.

She took stock of all her aches and pains. "Like I've been used as a punching bag."

"I know the feeling." Nick grimaced.

Heat crept up her neck. He'd experienced that just a few days ago.

"I was thinking about everything last night. We really need to get those SD cards to be able to prove our innocence. Maybe I got some images of Stella on the compound or involved with Las Sombras."

Alexis agreed. They didn't have much evidence now other than their word. It would be a game of he-said-she-said. Only there were two dead DEA agents so no one would believe them.

"Let's go get them."

Nick looked like he was going to argue but stopped and nodded.

They drove the damaged Las Sombras car to the compound. It was nice to be able to get around without having to use the snowmobile.

"The main entrance to the compound is guarded and we know the tunnel you used has been repaired. Our only hope is to find a weak spot in the fence," Nick said as he put the car in Park.

"Here's hoping we can find one," Alexis said, exiting the car.

They trudged through the snow looking for weak areas in the fence. Finally, they came across an area where an animal had dug under. A little more digging and it would be big enough for them to squeeze through. Nick got down on his hands and knees and dug deeper.

Once inside the compound, Nick and Alexis moved toward the building where he'd hidden the SD cards. As they drew nearer, they could see smoke puffs rising from somewhere in the compound. When they arrived at the building they had come to visit, Nick gasped.

"No."

"What?"

"The smoke is coming from the building I hid the SD cards in. I've got to get in there and save them before the building burns down."

"Why do you think it's on fire?"

"I can only assume they're trying to get rid of the evidence. A lot of the cutting took place there."

"Why would they burn it down? Won't that bring the fire department and police?"

"It's getting too dangerous. They're probably closing down and moving to another location." He looked around the area. "Stay hidden. I'll be back."

"It's too risky. What if you get stuck in there?" Worry gnawed at her middle.

"I won't. I know exactly where everything is. Stay here and stay hidden."

She nodded and crouched down behind the bushes. She watched him disappear into the building.

Movement to the right of the building caught her attention. Men were milling about.

They knew the building was on fire but weren't doing anything to put it out. As a matter of fact, a few men were holding red gas cans. They poured gas on the back side of the building while another man came by and lit it. They were destroying evidence. She had to get Nick out of there before he was collateral damage.

She waited until the men disappeared around the corner of the building and then raced to the front door. She opened the door and stepped inside. The main room was hazy with smoke. With as many fires as Las Sombras was starting, it wouldn't be long until the building was filled with smoke.

She used her coat sleeve and covered her mouth to try to control the amount of smoke she inhaled. She stepped deeper into the building searching for Nick. Her vision was hampered by plumes of smoke. Fire crackled from somewhere deep within the building's bowels. She swallowed the fear that crept up her throat. She had to get to Nick before the fire did. Or worse, Las Sombras.

The SD cards were in the room all the way at the end of the hall on the left. Nick raced down the hall. He'd chosen that room because it was scarcely used. There was less chance of someone accidentally coming across the SD cards. He'd hidden them in a vent above the door. The door to the room was closed. He used the back of his hand to test the door handle. Heat radiated from the knob as his hand got closer. He didn't need to feel it to know it was too hot to touch. He didn't dare open the door for fear of a back draft. That could be deadly.

He looked to the ceiling. Could he bust through the ceiling and reach the vent that way? Smoke was quickly filling the building. His lungs ached and he coughed. Whatever he did, his time was limited. He ran to the opposite room and found a chair. Back in the hallway, he stood on the chair and used a metal pipe he'd found to start tearing a hole in the drywall ceiling.

He coughed harder and harder. There was no use. He wasn't going to be able to get to those cards in time. Much longer and he'd succumb to smoke inhalation.

If he died in here, then he'd be leaving Alexis alone out there to fight this battle. He couldn't do that. She deserved better.

He dropped the pipe and hopped down off the chair. A hand grabbed his bicep. He spun around ready to fight, but it was Alexis standing next to him.

"What are you doing in here?" he asked.

"We've got to get out of here. They're using gasoline to start more fires around the building. We won't make it out of here if we don't go now."

He pushed her toward the front of the building and prayed they would make it out of the structure. It was dark and smoke filled his entire field of vision, disorienting him. He felt for the wall and followed it to the front of the building.

"Here's the door," Alexis said. She grunted. "It won't open."

He could hear her struggling. He pushed her to the side and grabbed the door and yanked with all of his might. Nothing. They were trapped.

"I left the door open when I came in," she cried before a coughing fit racked her body.

Someone must have closed the door and barred it from the outside. Las Sombras knew Nick and Alexis were in the building. This had been a trap.

He needed to find another way out.

"Come on." Nick grabbed her hand and pulled her to the first room in the hallway. The windows were covered by bars. He pulled her to the next room. More bars. All the rooms that they could access didn't provide an escape.

They were trapped.

"It's no use. We are going to die here." Alexis coughed.

They had come so far and lost so much and still there was nothing they could do. Everything they had done had been in vain. No one would know what happened to them. The authorities would just think they were on the run. The cartel would continue on like nothing else happened. They'd keep on hurting more people.

"Not if I can help it." Nick searched the building.

The smoke grew thicker and he began to cough. He used

his sleeve to cover his mouth and try to control the intake of the smoke. They were running out of time.

He grabbed a chair and threw it at the barred windows. The glass shattered but they would never escape the bars.

Nick had checked every room. Every room except the bathroom. Would it even have a window? He wouldn't know unless he looked.

Alexis leaned her back against the wall next to him and coughed. She slid down the wall until she was seated and put her head on her knees. She was giving up.

He left her there and raced to the bathroom. He coughed and his lungs spasmed for fresh air. He opened the bathroom door and ventured in. There. Above the toilet he could see light filtering in. He got closer and stood on the toilet. The window was barless. Finally, a way to escape.

TWELVE

"Alexis. Come on."

Nick helped her to a standing position. She couldn't get a deep breath. Her lungs were desperate for clean air and rejected each smoky inhalation. He ushered her into a small bathroom and closed the door. Huddling in here wasn't going to keep them safe. They had been trapped in the building on purpose. They were going to die. The men outside were probably watching the building and cheering on the flames.

"Alexis, look at me." He gripped her biceps. She looked at him through watery eyes. "That window is small enough for you to get out. I need you to get as far away from here as you can."

She shook her head. She wasn't going to leave him here to die. "I can't. You will die."

"If you don't, we'll both die and the investigation dies with us," he pleaded.

She shook her head again. He was sacrificing himself for her.

"Alexis, you have to do this. The cartel needs to be brought down and the only way that will happen is if one of us survives."

He stood up on the toilet, opened the small window and stepped down.

He helped her onto the toilet and gave her a boost through the window. Once her head was outside the window she gasped for fresh air. She started coughing even more as the fresh air filled her lungs. She scrambled to cover her mouth. She didn't need to draw attention to them.

Alexis scrambled the rest of the way out and landed on the ground. Her head pounded from the concussion and lack of oxygen, and her hip had never hurt this bad.

She waited in the snow and looked around, but no one came around. Had they set the fire and left, or were they watching the front door?

She had to do something. There was no way she was going to let Nick die. She'd already had to bury one man she cared about.

Alexis tiptoed around the front of the building. There were three Las Sombras men sitting on the hood of a car, watching the front door. Given all the other windows were barred, they probably figured there was no use watching from anywhere else.

What could she do? Nick wouldn't last much longer until smoke inhalation got him.

She had to get into the building or cause a distraction.

She raced to the back of the building and found what she was looking for. An older-model SUV was parked at the back. She ran to the driver's door. *Lord, please let it be unlocked.*

She tried the handle, and it was unlocked. *Thank You.*

Alexis climbed in and began looking for keys. She looked above the visor, and in the ignition, but there were no keys. Just when she was about to give up, she noticed keys tucked in the cup holder.

"Thank You, Lord."

She was going to have to work fast. She ran back to the bathroom window.

"Nick," she half yelled, half whispered. She didn't want to draw the attention of the men up front. She pounded her hand on the wall. "Nick."

"I told you to run." His face came into view in the window.

"We'll talk about that later. You need to get to the next room. I'm going to be opening the window for you."

"How—"

"Just do it." She ran back to the end of the building, opened the SUV door and started the engine.

She grabbed the rope that had been lying at the back of the building and tied it to the grille guard on the SUV. She drove to where the SUV was facing the barred window, climbed out of the car and tied the other end of the rope to the bars.

After making sure both knots were secure, she climbed back in the SUV, put it in Reverse and floored it.

She could hear the tires spinning, but she was getting no traction.

"Come on." She slapped the steering wheel.

Putting the vehicle in Drive, she went forward a little bit. Alexis turned the tires slightly, hoping to get better traction. She put the SUV in Reverse again and slammed on the gas. The tires slipped at first, but finally gained traction. The SUV lurched backward, the rope tightened and the bars popped off with a clang.

She put the car in Drive, watched and waited for Nick to come out of the building. There was no doubt the men up front heard what had happened and they would be here any minute.

Smoke poured from the opening. But Nick never came.

"No. No. No. Come on, Nick." She grasped the door handle and opened it, determined to go find him.

Shouting sounded before the men rounded the building. If Nick didn't hurry, she'd have no choice but to leave him. Something she didn't want to do.

Finally, he emerged.

He was coughing badly. He shuffled to the passenger's side and climbed in.

She threw the SUV in Drive and raced away from the building, toward the perimeter of the compound. Nick coughed consistently beside her. She reached over and patted him on the back. Not that it actually did any good, but it made her feel like she was helping.

"Why didn't you leave?" he asked between coughs.

"Would you have left me?"

Other than the coughing, Nick remained quiet.

"Thought so." She could see the fence coming up. She pressed the gas harder. "Hold on."

They crashed through the fence. She kept going, not bothering to slow down, and made her way toward the main road. Alexis gripped the wheel. The metal bars clanged as it was dragged behind the SUV.

"We need to get rid of this."

She pulled up next to the car they had used earlier and they quickly jumped in, Nick in the driver's seat. Nick gunned the engine and the tires spun but the car didn't move.

"We're stuck." Nick let off the gas.

No. They'd come so far. It couldn't end like this.

He put the car in Reverse and the car crept backward. He switched to Drive, turned the wheels and the car lurched from its spot and gained speed.

One crisis avoided.

A while later, Nick pulled the car behind the abandoned cabin. She walked into the cabin and he secured the door. Alexis spun around and asked the question Nick had been dreading since escaping the fire.

"Did you get the SD cards?" Hope filled her eyes.

He shook his head and watched her face fall. "They were in the room the fire started in."

"So, this all was for nothing?" Her shoulders slumped.

He nodded.

"Do you have another copy somewhere? Did you save them to the cloud? Please tell me we have something else that will bring down the cartel." Panic laced her voice.

He shook his head. "We are back at square one."

He should have tried harder. Now everything was lost.

Not only did they not have anything to bring down the cartel, but also he was now wanted by the police for the murder of two federal agents and the cartel wanted him for stealing missing drugs. And Alexis was wanted along with him.

If he had forced her to stay, he probably would've had to tie her up to keep her from following him. Plus she saved his life on the compound despite him telling her to run. For that, he would be forever grateful.

"Thank you for saving me back there."

She nodded. "It's what you would've done."

The ache in his leg grew worse as time went on. His chest burned from inhaling all the smoke. He just wanted to lie down and sleep until everything was over. Let someone else deal with this.

But he couldn't do that. He was the only one who could end this. If he gave up now, things would only get worse. More innocent people would die. He'd be lying if he said giving up and disappearing didn't have an appeal. They could go their separate ways and start their lives over. Cover their tracks, lie low.

But he couldn't do that. He was a man of honor and integrity. Nick was committed to this mission. She depended on him like Tony had. He was *not* going to fail her.

Alexis coughed. Her lungs no doubt felt like his. They should both seek medical treatment, but where could they go? Who could they trust?

A crash sounded from outside, making Alexis jump.

Something was outside the cabin. "It's probably just that bear," he said to ease Alexis's fear, but he wasn't completely confident in that answer. He crossed to the front door and peeked out the tiny window.

A shadow passed, not big enough to be a bear but definitely the size of a man. It was over in front of the main building. He saw two other men spread out from there and make their way to the surrounding cabins.

Searching for them.

He turned back to Alexis. "We're not alone here. There are people searching the cabins. They must have followed us from the compound. We need to get out of here fast."

He removed the blockade from the front door and opened it slightly, scanning the surroundings in front of their cabin. He didn't see anybody or any footprints other than the ones that they'd left.

Nick grabbed her hand and opened the door. They sneaked around to the back of the building where the car had been parked.

He said, "Once we start that motor they're going to know where we are. We're going to have to go fast. You need to drive, and I'll provide cover."

He pulled his gun out. She waited until he was in the car before starting the engine.

He rolled down the window and readied the gun. "Go!"

She revved the motor and took off just as a man rounded the front of the cabin. The man fired a shot and glass shattered. Nick returned fire.

"Nick," Alexis said.

"I'm fine, keep going." Nick kept an eye for more shooters.

Several men rounded the main cabin. More shots rang out followed by a loud pop. The car jerked to the right. They'd lost a tire. As long as the car moved, it didn't matter right now. They could deal with it when they weren't in the middle of a gun battle.

Alexis turned sharply onto the main road. The car fishtailed, the rear skidding to the right.

Alexis let off the gas and slightly turned the wheel to the right. Once the car straightened out, she pressed the accelerator. The car sped along the road. The sounds of gunfire were replaced with thumping coming from the front passenger's side.

How far could they make it?

What was the best decision? Pushing forward and risking a wreck, or being spotted by the local police and getting stopped, or ditching the car and taking off on foot? The farther away from Las Sombras they got, the better. But the farther from them they got, the closer to city limits they'd be. Ditching the car appeared to be the better option.

"As soon as you can, pull over. We need to get rid of the car. It won't be long until they're on our tail and we'll never outrun them with a busted tire."

Nick kept an eye on the side mirror, watching for company.

Alexis slowed and turned onto a private driveway.

"Pull up a ways so the car can't be seen from the road," Nick instructed.

Alexis stopped the car and looked at the clock on the radio. "We're supposed to meet Declan in an hour."

"We'll make it." They had to make it. It was their only hope.

They abandoned the car and trudged through the snowy forest, staying close to the road but keeping hidden. They couldn't afford to be spotted or to get lost in the woods.

"Where'd you learn to drive like that?" Nick asked. He was impressed with the way Alexis had handled the fishtailing and recovery.

Alexis stuffed her hands in her pockets. "My dad grew up in these Colorado mountains. Taught me how to drive in the snow and ice even though we didn't have much where we lived in Arkansas. But he wanted me to know how. Plus, that knowledge came in handy when traveling the back road and doing doughnuts in old fields."

"Oh, you were a wild one." He wasn't sure he could imagine Alexis out causing havoc. "I didn't take you for a risk taker."

She paused a beat. "Only when it comes to my heart."

Nick didn't know how to respond.

"I dated a guy who was into it. We didn't last long. Then I met Tony. He was the last time I risked my heart."

Would she risk her heart again? Did she think he was a risk worth taking?

THIRTEEN

Nick went silent after her proclamation. What was he thinking? She wanted to ask him, to know what was going on inside his head. But she wouldn't. Now wasn't the time. They had a mission and needed to stick to it.

Traffic on the road had picked up, which meant they were getting closer to town. They were making good time. Or at least she thought they were. She didn't have a watch anymore.

Nick held his arm out and stopped her. "We're coming up on town. We need to keep our heads down and be quick. We can't afford to be caught."

She knew that. She also knew he was just trying to do his job. They walked in silence. A maroon sedan slowed as it approached them. Alexis's muscles tensed. She kept her focus on the sidewalk in front of her.

Don't look.

The car passed and she relaxed a little.

Rocks crunched as the hood of the maroon sedan pulled up equal to them. Her heart skittered in her chest. She heard whirring as a window was rolled down.

Nick grabbed her arm and yanked her behind him. He put himself between her and whoever was in the car.

"I thought that was you," came a man's voice from inside the car.

Nick took slow steady steps backward. His body bumped into her. She matched his retreat. Preparing to run.

"Relax. I'm not wanting to cause trouble."

Nick maintained his protective stance.

"I'm going to get out of the car so we can talk."

Nick grabbed her hand and squeezed it. Was he preparing her to run?

Alexis peeked around him and watched as the deputy from yesterday exited the vehicle. "Let's get out of sight." The deputy limped toward a shaded area.

"Looks like you didn't have any serious damage from being pinned," Nick said, slowly following the deputy.

"Nothing is broken. Just bumps and bruises. I didn't get a chance to say thank you for saving my life. After what happened yesterday, I believe you."

Nick relaxed a little. His grip on her hand loosened but he didn't let go.

"They've got an all-points bulletin out on you two. You guys need to skip town."

"Why are you helping us?" Alexis asked, stepping up shoulder to shoulder with Nick.

The man looked at her; compassion softened his features. "Because he saved my life. And something isn't right. I can't put my finger on it, but the sheriff has been acting weird since this all started. I'll give you a ten-minute head start and then call in a spotting across town." He turned and limped back to the car.

Nick pulled her forward. The park was only a couple of blocks away. Alexis shivered and wrapped the coat tighter around her as it came into view. Her side burned and her legs were weary. She wasn't sure how much longer she would be able to go on. Her body had been through a lot. How much more could she take?

This meeting with Nick's friend terrified her. Were they walking into yet another trap?

"Are you sure we can trust this guy Declan?"

Nick took her hand. "I think it's a chance we need to take. We can't do anything else on our own."

She prayed it wasn't a trap.

A family of four were swinging at the playground and a group of people were playing basketball on the other end of the park. The snow did not stop outdoor adventures here.

In the middle of the park, next to the bathrooms, a man sat on the picnic table.

"Is that him?" She nodded toward the man, not wanting to draw attention by pointing.

"Yes." Nick did not look directly at him. "Let's walk by and circle back around."

They followed the walking trail that circled the perimeter of the park until they reached the opposite side. The man stood and started walking toward them. Nick wrapped an arm around her and pulled her close, careful not to jostle her. Her heart beat a rapid staccato in her chest. Her fight-or-flight reflex was gearing up for action.

"Nick." The man held out his hand for a shake.

Nick gave the man a firm shake. "Declan."

"You must be Alexis." He held out his hand for her.

She didn't accept. She was weary of all strangers. Especially if they were DEA.

"You look like you've seen better days." Declan scanned the park. "We need to make this quick. Feds are crawling all over the place."

"Looking for us?"

"Your names and photos are plastered all over the news. You're wanted for the murder of two DEA agents. I got to admit I was shocked when the BOLO went out on you. I never pegged you as dirty," Declan said.

"What exactly are they saying?"

"The story right now is that you retired from the agency and started working for Las Sombras. Blackstone found you, and you killed both him and Tek Ford. Although the reason for Ford's death isn't clear."

Nick groaned. "I didn't retire. Blackstone sent me undercover. I was gathering information to bring Las Sombras down. Tony believed there was a mole in the local office and when he died within a day of telling me, I was convinced he was right. I've been looking for someone in the agency working for them ever since then. At least that's what I thought I was doing."

"It's not looking so good for you." Declan shook his head. "They've got surveillance footage of you on the compound and working with Las Sombras."

"Of course they do," Nick muttered. "I was working undercover."

"Do you have any proof?" Declan asked.

"All the evidence I'd collected was intercepted and the backups I made were destroyed in a fire."

"So, it's your word against a dead guy."

Nick nodded.

They were fighting an impossible battle. The evidence was gone and the people who had answers were dead. Except for Stella Ford.

"We need to look at Stella Ford," Alexis said.

Declan looked at her.

"I originally thought her husband was responsible for my husband's death. But she confessed to his murder right before she tried to suffocate me."

Declan looked at her. "Why'd you think she killed your husband?"

"I asked her if her husband had been suspicious about a mole or if he'd noticed anything out of the ordinary." Alexis swallowed the lump in her throat. "The car wreck that killed Tony happened the next day."

Declan took a moment to ponder what she said. "So you think since you said something to her, she then told her husband and that alerted them to Tony's suspicions?"

She nodded.

"But Tek Ford was thoroughly investigated and deemed not to be the leak," Nick said, finishing the story for her. "Then Alexis spotted Stella on the compound."

"We decided to visit Tek and see if he knew anything about what his wife was up to."

"But we didn't get very far before someone took him out," Nick supplied. "Probably Stella herself, since we know she's a murderer."

"So we have a DEA agent's wife possibly working with the cartel, and a dead DEA agent who sent you on a rogue undercover investigation." Declan stared off into the distance. "Do you think maybe Blackstone also thought there was a mole in the agency, and he came up with this retirement/undercover assignment hoping to flush out the real mole?"

"I don't know what to think." Nick folded his arms over his chest. "Blackstone is dead so we can't ask him. And my operation was off the books, so there is nobody else in the agency to ask. Right now, finding Stella Ford is our only lead."

Declan pulled a plastic card from his pocket and handed it to Nick.

"I took the liberty of renting a motel room. I wasn't sure how this was going to go down, but I believe you. Take this key card. It's for a hotel outside the city. There's a blue sedan in the parking lot and the keys are in it. There will be supplies in the hotel room. Go lay low. Let me dig around a little bit and see what I can find out."

A police cruiser slowly drove by the park. It was time to wrap this meeting up and get to that hotel room.

"Thank you." Declan would never know how much Nick appreciated his help.

He helped Alexis to the car and pointed it in the direction of the hotel. Everything was falling apart. All of their leads kept dying. The evidence had been destroyed. They were back at square one. Not even at square one. Could you even go further back, past square one?

"I don't want to sound like a broken record but are you sure we can trust Declan?" Alexis said, buckling her seat belt.

"Declan isn't involved in this. He's been hundreds of miles away and has no connections here."

"Other than you," Alexis said.

"Other than me," he huffed.

"I'm just trying to understand. Right now you're the only person I trust implicitly."

"Not only did Declan and I go through training together, but we worked several dangerous cases in the early days. He saved my life more than once." Nick rubbed the back of his neck. "I'm alive today because of him."

Alexis turned to face him in her seat.

Nick swallowed. "We were undercover working our way up the supply chain of a drug ring in Milwaukee. We staged a drug buy. I was the purchaser and Declan was my eyes. He saw a friend of the dealer sneaking up on me. Stopped the man before he could put a bullet in my head."

Alexis reached over and squeezed his hand. "Okay."

Nick parked the car directly in front of the hotel room. Using the key card, he unlocked the hotel suite Declan had secured for them. He made Alexis wait right inside the door while he cleared the suite. He wanted to trust Declan. Had no reason not to, but the last couple of days had taught him not to let his guard down.

"Clear," he called from the bedroom. He walked into the small living area.

Alexis stood at the door, her arms wrapped around her

midsection. She was pale. She needed a comfortable rest. She was rubbing her fist on her hip again. She was going to end up overdoing it and making her condition worse.

He crossed the room and rubbed his hands up and down her arms. "Why don't you do those exercises you need and maybe lay down for a bit?"

She nodded. "I think I will."

She started to unzip her coat but her fingers fumbled. She finally grasped the zipper and got it undone. She must have made a wrong move because pain etched her face.

"Here."

He helped slide the coat off and threw it on the couch. He leaned down and placed a soft kiss on her forehead. "I'll be in the living room if you need me."

He left the door open a crack. He wanted her to have peace and quiet but he also wanted to be able to hear her if she were to need help. She'd been through a lot and her body had taken a beating in recent days.

He spotted a black duffel bag sitting on the coffee table. Declan had said he'd left some supplies for them. He opened the bag and began unloading the items onto the table. There were two cell phones, a gun and ammunition, cash, first aid kit and some protein bars. This would be good for now but it wouldn't last long. How had it come to this? He had always been on the *good* side of the law and now he was getting a glimpse of what being on the run was really like, despite being innocent.

A few hours later Nick heard Alexis scream and ran to check on her. He realized she must have been having a nightmare.

"Alexis. Calm down. You're safe."

She sat up and threw her arms around him. "It was so real." She squeezed him tightly. He wrapped his arms around her and rubbed her back.

"It was just a nightmare. You're safe. I've got you."

"It wasn't a nightmare—it was a flashback. To the day Tony died. There was so much blood. The car tumbled down the embankment. I remember hearing glass breaking. When the car came to rest, Tony was pinned. He was bleeding. I could tell he had serious internal damage. Still, he told me everything was going to be okay. He was keeping me calm. Before delirium took over, the last thing he said to me was, 'I love you so much. Have Nick clean the cabin vents.'"

Nick abruptly pulled away. "What did he say?"

Adrenaline soared through his body. Good ol' Tony left him something. This could all be over soon.

FOURTEEN

Alexis wiped the tears from her eyes and gave a half-hearted chuckle. "It was so weird. He must have been out of it."

Nick placed both hands on her face. His eyes were intense. "Tell me again."

A chill inched its way up her spine. "He said to tell you to clean the vents."

Nick jumped to his feet. "That's it." He disappeared from the room.

"What's it?"

Nick came back into the room with a pile of clothing and handed it to her.

"Declan brought us some clothes. The bathroom is fully stocked. Why don't you get cleaned up?"

She was just as confused now as she had been when Tony had said it. "What did Tony mean?"

"It was a code for me."

"Code?"

"Yes. We had done a few undercover operations together. We needed a way to communicate with each other without anyone knowing what was going on. We had to find a way to pass information. Tony would always cough or sneeze, then complain about his allergies and say someone needed to clean the vents. That's when I knew there was something he needed me to find. The information would be hidden in a vent somewhere."

"So, you think maybe he has evidence that could help us hidden in a vent at my cabin?"

"That's what we're going to find out once you're ready."

"What about Las Sombras? Do you think they're watching the cabin? I mean they found us at that abandoned ski resort cabin. The only other place they know about for us is my cabin."

"It's definitely a possibility. We'll need to be careful and be quick."

Alexis was silent on the ride to the cabin. This whole time she'd held the answer to their problems and didn't even know it. Now they were headed back to the cabin. The cabin that had memories both good and bad. Would they find what they needed? Could this really all be over?

She looked at Nick. He was focused on the road.

She remembered the way he tenderly kissed her forehead as she drifted off to sleep. Surely something he meant innocently felt more important to her than it did to him. She'd always loved forehead kisses. To her, that was a special moment of tenderness and caring. Something deeper than just attraction. Was that something Nick gave thought to? Or was it just an action to help calm her?

It didn't really matter. Once this was all over they would go their separate ways. The cartel would be brought down, and Tony's murderers would be punished. It wouldn't absolve her of all her guilt, but it would definitely lighten the load.

Nick would go back to his life as a DEA agent, risking his life to bring the world's bad guys down. He'd forget about her. Meanwhile, she'd go back to what? She wouldn't have anything left. What she'd been living for the past year would have been accomplished.

"Everything okay?" Nick reached over and tapped her forearm.

"I was thinking that I had the answer this entire time."

If only she had understood. She could've told Nick sooner. They wouldn't be fighting this battle right now. But he was sent undercover and stopped all contact with her.

He grabbed her hand. "It's not your fault."

"How can you say that? It's my fault Tony's dead. And I kept his last words to myself because I thought he was delirious," she cried.

He'd had severe injuries and was no doubt in serious pain. She'd just thought he didn't know what he was saying.

"What's important is now we know. Now we can move forward. Find what he left and put an end to all of this." He gently squeezed her hand.

Nick pulled the car into the driveway in front of the cabin and shut off the engine.

She opened the car door, and together they climbed the porch steps.

The cabin door was unlocked.

Nick pulled out a gun.

"Stay behind me."

He opened the door, sweeping the weapon from left to right as he cleared the front room.

"Wait right there." He disappeared into the different rooms of the cabin before coming back to meet her. "The cabin is clear."

"What are we looking for?" Alexis didn't know what kind of evidence Tony would have left behind.

"Hopefully something that will help close this mystery."

"So, whatever we're looking for is going to be in a vent?"

"Yes." Nick pulled out a phone and switched on a flashlight app. "We'll start in the bedroom."

"I'll get the step stool."

Alexis walked down the small hallway to the closet she had been hiding in just days before. She opened the door and grabbed the step stool, then hurried back to the bedroom.

Nick climbed the step stool and aimed the flashlight into the vent.

"See anything?"

He shook his head. "Nothing here." He backed down. "We'll keep looking."

Alexis followed him to the bathroom, where he repeated the process.

"Nothing there."

She trailed behind him as he checked the vents in the front room, laundry room, hallway and finally the kitchen. Her hope deflated with each empty vent they found.

Nick let out an exasperated breath as he leaned his hip against the counter. "Nothing."

"Maybe Tony really was delirious." Alexis blew out a breath. "Maybe he was confused and was just talking about random things. Getting things mixed up."

"Do you really believe that?" Nick asked. "Had he been coherent up until that statement?"

"Yes. He'd remained clearheaded until he took his last breath." A tear rolled down her cheek.

"It's okay." Nick reached out and wiped it away with the pad of his thumb. "I just haven't looked in the right vent yet."

Nick didn't want her to feel any worse, but maybe Tony had been delirious. Maybe there wasn't anything here to be found. He looked at each of the vents in each room. He could check the dryer vent, but surely Tony wouldn't hide anything in there. He would think the moisture would ruin the evidence.

"Is there anything you want to get while we're here?" Even if they didn't find any evidence, it wouldn't be a wasted trip if Alexis was able to get stuff she needed.

"I'd like to get some of my own clothes."

"Why don't you go pack a bag and I'll keep looking?"

Alexis left the room.

Maybe Nick hadn't looked hard enough. Maybe he should get a screwdriver to take down all the faceplates to the vents, reach his hands in and see if he could feel anything. No. He knew what he saw; every vent was empty.

He looked around the kitchen. It was a small, modest kitchen. One like you would expect to find in a cabin in the woods. Stainless steel refrigerator, small stainless steel dishwasher. An older oven but the hood vent above the oven was new. Hood vent.

Nick went over to the stove, craned his head under the hood vent and shone the flashlight up. He couldn't see much. He stuck his hand up into the hood vent and loosened the grate over the vent.

He wasn't able to see what he was doing as he felt around blindly. The grate fell and clanked against the stove top. He lay on the stove top, twisted and shone the flashlight into the opening.

Aha. An envelope was stuffed up in the vent.

"Alexis, I got it," he shouted.

She didn't respond. He pulled the envelope from its hiding spot. It was fairly thick.

He debated on whether to open it now, or wait for her to come back. She'd been gone too long and hadn't responded to him. Something was wrong. Nick stuck the envelope under his arm and walked into the front room.

"I knew it was only a matter of time before you two came back." Stella Ford stood at the cabin door, a gun aimed at him. Alexis was sitting on the couch.

Stella pulled a pair of handcuffs from her pocket and threw them at Alexis.

They landed on the floor in front of her.

"Cuff him. Don't do anything funny." She aimed the gun at Nick.

Nick could see the determination and cold-bloodedness in Stella's eyes. He knew she meant business.

Alexa picked up the cuffs and walked slowly until she was standing in front of him. He stuck his wrists out together for her to cuff.

"No, not that way. Hands behind his back."

Nick turned around slowly and put his hands behind his back. The cold metal clamped on his wrists.

"Now be a good girl and take his weapon. I want the magazine ejected and the chamber cleared."

Nick stiffened. Right now, Alexis stood between him and the bullet. Anything he tried to do would end her life.

"Do it," he told Alexis.

She lifted his shirt and pulled the gun from its holster and proceeded to do as Stella had said.

"Good," Stella said. "Now throw everything into the fireplace."

Normally it wouldn't be a good idea to heat up ammunition, but the cabin had been unoccupied for a couple of days and the fire had died out.

"Now both of you have a seat on the couch."

They did as they were instructed. Stella walked over and stood in front of Nick with the gun in her right hand. She pulled the envelope from under his arm.

"We knew there had to be more evidence somewhere." Stella waved the gun around the room. "You can't expect to have DEA agents investigating and not have multiple backups."

"Now what?" Nick asked.

They needed to keep Stella talking. Maybe he could find out enough information to bring down the cartel if they could escape. If she talked long enough maybe he could come up with a plan.

"Now we wait."

"Wait for what?" Alexis asked. She sat up straighter. "You already killed my husband and probably yours too. And another DEA agent is dead. You got everything you want. Nobody can prove anything. What's left?"

Stella laughed, a cross between maniacal and evil. "Sweetheart, you don't know anything."

Stella was right about that. "Why don't you tell us what we don't know?" Nick asked.

"I'm not stupid." Stella rolled her eyes. "This is not where I'm going to confess the whole big plan to you right before I kill you."

"You're not in charge." Nick leaned back against the couch. "You're just some lackey Las Sombras has doing their bidding. Here waiting on the boss. Which means you probably don't know what the big plan is."

Stella's jaw ticked. It struck a nerve.

Nick continued, "So, what? You do the dirty work and they get the rewards. What have they promised you?"

"You two really are dense." She shook her head.

Alexis gently elbowed him. Did she have a plan?

"Enlighten us because as I see it you are just some small fish in a big pond." Nick was hoping to fluster Stella. Then he could make his move. "Doing their bidding. Following directions. Not taking care of things on your own. Is that what it is? They don't trust you to make decisions?"

"You don't know what you're talking about." Stella sneered, "I am no small fish." She relaxed a little, letting down her guard.

Alexis jumped from the couch and tackled Stella in the midsection, sending them both to the ground. Stella kept control of the gun. She brought it up to shoot Alexis, but Alexis was waiting and grabbed her hand.

The two women wrestled over the gun. Nick couldn't see what was going on.

A gunshot rang out and both women went still.

Nick's head pounded and his heart ached as he saw blood pool beneath the women.

He jumped from the couch and knelt next to the two women. "Alexis!"

No. She couldn't die. Not now. He couldn't fail again.

FIFTEEN

Nick's voice was barely audible over the ringing in her ears.

Alexis lay on her back. Stella's limp body was on top of her. Alexis pulled the gun out of Stella's reach and rolled Stella off of her.

Nick was kneeling next to them. "Are you okay?"

She nodded. She was okay physically and she was okay emotionally and mentally for now, but once the adrenaline wore off she would probably fall apart. It had been an accident. She hadn't meant for Stella to die. But she couldn't have let Stella kill them either.

"Good. Now help me get out of these." Nick turned around and waved his cuffed hands at her.

She nodded and went into the bedroom, where she pulled out the universal handcuff key Tony had kept around the house. She did not want to rifle through Stella's pockets.

She unlocked the cuffs and freed Nick. He immediately wrapped her in a tight hug.

"Thank God you're okay. Let's get out of here and see what Tony left for us."

He grabbed the envelope Tony had left him and then took Alexis's hand and pulled her to the cabin door. She numbly followed.

They rushed to the car and piled in. Nick handed her the envelope. "See what's in there."

Alexis tore open the envelope.

"What is it?" Nick pulled the car out of the driveway.

Her hands shook. "It's a list. Select dates, times and addresses." She didn't recognize any of the addresses, but

Nick probably would, given he'd been undercover with Las Sombras for months.

"What else is there?"

She thumbed through the documents. More lists. A few pictures of people she didn't recognize. She stopped on a picture of Stella Ford with a person who wore a hoodie. Alexis couldn't tell if it was a man or a woman. There were several more pictures, but none of them showed the person's face.

She continued flipping through the documents. There were photos of vehicles coming in and out of the compound, and the compound itself. Nothing that made sense to her.

"There are photos here. I don't recognize anybody other than Stella. Maybe you could look through them and see if you recognize them."

"I will once we're back at the hotel."

A little later, Nick parked the car and they hurried to their room, where they sat at the small table. Alexis watched as Nick pored over the documents. He separated them into piles.

"This is definitely information on the cartel. Looks like a list of rendezvous points. Probably some major drug trading happening. The photos of the people whose faces we can see I recognize as all cartel members. The vehicle plates and things I don't recognize, but we could give it to Declan, have him run the plates and see what he can come up with."

"Have you heard from Declan since the park?"

Nick shook his head. He pulled out his phone and sent a text message, then started taking photos of the information they'd found.

"Hopefully he'll respond soon."

"Stella was our only lead and now she's dead."

The situation felt helpless. It was like they would take a step forward and fall two steps back. They weren't ever going to get this figured out. Would they spend the rest of their life on the run, looking over their shoulders, waiting for a cartel member to find them? Or the police? They were wanted for crimes they didn't commit. But there was no way to prove their innocence.

She looked at Nick still intently poring over the information. He wouldn't give up though. She knew that. He would keep going and keep pressing on until this had a resolution.

Nick had scoured the information they had found. There was a lot of material there, and given the resources the DEA had they'd be able to bring the cartel down with it. A part of the puzzle had been solved. Stella was the mole. Nick doubted Tek was involved, except as someone to take the blame. He'd been fully vetted and cleared.

"What was Stella's connection to the cartel? And was she connected to any other DEA agents?" Nick voiced his thoughts.

"Maybe we could find something that can connect her to another agent or point us in the right direction at her house."

"I don't know that we would find anything. Her house is a crime scene. The police have already searched it."

"But they were looking for stuff relating to Tek's death. We're not looking for that," Alexis reasoned.

"I'm not so sure she would have stuff in her house. I mean she was married to a DEA agent and as far as we know he had no clue she was working with the cartel."

"Possibly. But also if he worked a lot of undercover missions she'd be home alone a lot." Alexis stood and grimaced as she did.

"Are you feeling up to it?" He was concerned about her.

"I'll be fine. I'll be even better when this is all over."

Nick's phone buzzed on the table. He looked at the caller ID, which showed a preprogrammed number for Declan.

"Hello."

"You said you wanted me to call."

"Yeah. We found some information hidden in Tony's cabin. It's enough to bring down the cartel. Stella Ford was the mole. But we don't know how she got her information. And I don't think anyone is going to believe she was involved."

"Is she talking?" Declan asked.

"No. She's dead." Nick sighed.

"How?"

"She was holding us at gunpoint, Alexis tried to get the gun away from her, there was a struggle and the gun discharged, killing Stella. Now we need more solid proof since we can't corroborate it with her. There are photos of license plates that, if we could run, might bring us a clue."

"Shoot me some pictures and I'll see what I can do."

"Will do. Have you been able to find out anything on your end?" Nick was curious about what the story was at headquarters.

"Nothing we don't know already. Blackstone is dead. You're wanted for his murder. Tek is dead. You're wanted for his murder."

"Great."

It was anything but great. They'd actually killed Stella, the one death they could be charged for, and no one was even talking about it. Until they found her body at the cabin.

"Don't give up just yet. I'm still digging."

"We're going to head over to Stella Ford's house and see what we can find. She appears in several of these photos."

"Do you recognize anyone else?" Declan asked.

"Only those people from the cartel and Stella. Nobody else related to the agency."

"I'll keep digging. Call if you need anything."

"All right, thank you." Nick hung up the phone.

The Ford house was across town. Nick parked the borrowed car a block away from the house. He'd searched the area and didn't see anyone watching the house, but he still didn't want to draw any unnecessary attention to them.

He turned to Alexis. "We'll walk from here." The snow was beginning to melt on the road and sidewalks were wet. There was no crime scene tape across the door. The police had gathered their evidence and released the scene.

Nick tried the doorknob on the off chance that it was unlocked, but it wasn't. He looked around the porch trying to find where an extra key might've been hidden. He didn't want to have to break and enter if at all possible.

"You were friends with Stella. Do you know if she had a key hidden somewhere?"

She scrunched up her face. "I thought we were friends. She never mentioned an extra key to me."

He scanned the porch one more time. His gaze latched on to an odd-looking rock right off the porch step. He bent down and picked it up. Sure enough. It was a fake rock that held the key. He unlocked the door. They slipped in and shut the door behind them.

"Where do we start?" she asked.

"We start in the office, if there is one, and the bedroom."

People tended to hide their information in spaces they felt the safest. Their sanctuary. And the majority of people felt safest in their bedrooms. People always hid stuff in nightstands, under the bed or in closets. That's where they would look first.

The master bedroom was spacious with a king-size bed, chest of drawers, armoire and an entertainment center.

"You check that nightstand and I'll check this one."

They split up and began their search.

He found various odds and ends, coins, nail clippers, bills and books, but nothing that would help them with this case. He moved on to the dresser.

His search still turned up nothing. Alexis searched right along with him. They went through the armoire, the closet, between the box springs and mattress. Alexis disappeared into the bathroom while he crawled on the floor and looked under the bed.

"I found something," Alexis called from the bathroom.

He met her at the bathroom door. He could tell by the look on her face that something was wrong. Whatever she had found was not good.

"What is it?"

"Want to tell me why Stella Ford has a bill for a storage unit in your name?" She held out an envelope.

"What?"

He took the envelope from her and opened it. There was a key and a bill for a storage unit at the local storage facility with his name but Stella's address.

"I don't know anything about this." He flipped the bill over and found four numbers scrawled across the back. Must be the entry pin.

"Why would Stella open a storage unit in your name? Did you even know Stella?"

"No. I had never met her before. I have had a few encounters with Tek but that's as far as my relationship with the Fords goes."

"Maybe we should see what's in that storage unit. But first, I found this phone stashed with the envelope." She handed him the phone.

"Where did you find these?" He powered on the phone.

"In the box with her nail polishes," she said with a shrug.

He browsed through the phone contacts. There weren't any names or at least no real names. He scanned through the text messages. They were mostly setting up meets. Giving dates and prices. There was one longer string of text messages. As he scrolled through, it became apparent that Stella was carrying on an extramarital affair with whoever it was she had listed as D.

He opened the gallery and thumbed through the pictures,

several selfies. Then he found photos like the ones Tony had taken of the compound. He stopped on one picture, and everything he thought he knew unraveled.

"I know who the mole is, and it wasn't just Stella."

Alexis stepped closer to get a look at the phone. "Who?"

He turned the phone toward her.

"That's Blackstone." She looked at him, bewildered. "But he's dead now."

"They both are."

It had been Blackstone all along. He'd trusted that man and had been completely betrayed.

"This explains why the agency believes I retired and the mission he sent me on was me going to work for them." Nick rubbed his hand through his hair. "But it doesn't make sense. Why send me on an undercover mission looking for a mole in the agency when he was the mole?"

"Maybe to get you out of the way? Or so he could keep tabs on you?" She shrugged.

"Well, he's dead now so we'll never know." He stuffed the phone in his pocket with the envelope.

"Let's keep looking around. Maybe we'll find more."

They finished searching the house and couldn't find anything else incriminating.

"Let's check out that storage unit." They slipped from the Ford house and headed for the car.

A while later Nick pulled up to the locked gate of the storage facility. A keypad stood sentry. He looked at the bill again and punched in the four digits. The box beeped and the gate slowly opened. He eased the car through the gate and drove down the aisle searching for the unit number that was in his name.

"There it is." Alexis pointed to a unit on the right. It was set in a row of medium-sized units. Probably ten feet by twenty feet. He drove up the aisle and turned around. He wanted their car facing the exit for a quick getaway should they need it.

He took the key from the envelope and unlocked the padlock to the unit. He braced himself for what he was about to find. He opened the door. Shock reverberated through him. The possibilities of what could be behind the door had been running through his mind but he hadn't expected anything of this magnitude.

Alexis gasped. There were hundreds of brick-sized packages stacked waist high along the walls of the unit.

"Looks like we found the cartel's missing drugs."

"Definitely. About two million dollars' worth of product."

"No wonder the cartel is hot on your tail." That was a lot of money.

"I didn't take the drugs." Nick sighed.

"I know that, but they don't." Heat crept up her neck. She hadn't meant to insinuate he had stolen them. "I just meant they think you have two million dollars that belongs to them."

"I know."

"We need to call someone." She didn't want to have anything to do with the drugs.

"Yeah okay. 'Hello, my name is Nick Anderson. I have found a storage unit in my name with illegal drugs in it,'" Nick said in a mocking tone. "You expect to call someone and tell them that and not get arrested? We're already wanted for the murder of two DEA agents."

Nick closed the unit back up and wiped his prints from the doorknob and the lock. She didn't think that wiping them down would do tremendous good if they had video of them entering the storage facility and opening the unit.

"Do they have video cameras? Maybe we could see who's been using it."

"I don't know. Let's get out of here and then find out." Nick appeared anxious to get away. She didn't blame him. She didn't want to be anywhere near these drugs. Especially since the cartel had a target on Nick's back.

Nick pulled the car through the gate after using the sleeve of his shirt to wipe the box after he entered the passcode. Then he pulled off to the side and pulled out the cell phone Declan had given him and dialed a number.

"Good afternoon. I have a storage unit and I think someone has been in it and moved stuff around. Do you have cameras watching the units?"

Alexis could only hear Nick's side of the conversation.

"Okay. Thanks." His voice held a hint of irritation. "No. It's okay. Probably just my wife went in looking for something and didn't tell me. Thanks for your help." He hung up.

"I'm guessing they don't have cameras," Alexis said.

"Only on the entrance. Not on the units."

Nick dialed another number. This time he put the phone on speaker.

"Declan," he explained.

The call was answered on the second ring.

"It's Nick. We found something huge." He skipped the pleasantries.

"What's that?" Declan shuffled something in the background.

"I just found a storage unit with the cartel's missing drugs."

"That's great." Excitement filled Declan's voice. "How much?"

"I'd say around two million dollars." Nick ran his hand through his hair.

"Are you serious?" Declan asked.

"Dead. But we have a problem." Nick fidgeted with the steering wheel cover. "The unit was opened in my name."

Declan let out a low whistle.

"What are you going to do about the drugs?"

"I haven't figured that out yet."

"Okay. Keep me updated." Declan said goodbye and hung up.

"What about that deputy?" Alexis asked from the passenger's seat.

"What about him?"

"Can he help us? He said he believed us and that something weird was going on with the sheriff's department." She was grasping but there had to be an ally for them somewhere.

"I don't know. I'm pretty sure there's a local cop on Las Sombras's payroll."

"But Deputy Wheeler could have arrested us but he also could've turned us over to Las Sombras if he was the leak," Alexis said.

"It's worth a shot."

He dialed the police department's phone number and looked out the windshield. "I need to speak with Deputy Wheeler."

Alexis listened to Nick's side of the conversation with Deputy Wheeler. They agreed to meet at the storage facility in twenty minutes.

"I want to park the car outside the facility and walk in. It will let us stay hidden and be able to watch and see if anyone else comes with Deputy Wheeler. Make sure we're not being set up. If it's a trap, they won't know we're here and we can get out without being seen."

They found a location that kept them hidden but allowed them to see the entrance of the facility. A police cruiser drove up to the keypad. Alexis recognized Deputy Wheeler as the driver. He entered the four-digit code Nick had given him. The gate opened, he pulled in and waited for the gate to close behind him. Then he drove down the main aisle headed to the aisle with the drug unit. He pulled up to the unit, stepped out of his cruiser and looked up and down the aisle. Alexis couldn't see anyone else in the cruiser. Deputy Wheeler inspected the door to the unit holding the drugs.

Nick waited a few minutes, while he rotated his attention between Deputy Wheeler and the entry gate.

"I'm satisfied he's alone." Nick grabbed her hand and together they walked toward the deputy.

Deputy Wheeler turned abruptly, his hand resting on his holster, and stared at them.

"It's just us." Nick raised their joined hands.

Deputy Wheeler relaxed. "I was beginning to wonder if you were going to show up."

"Forgive me but it's been a long several days and we're not exactly sure who to trust."

"Understandable." Deputy Wheeler nodded. "So you say you found out someone rented this unit in your name and stuffed it with cartel drugs?"

"Yes. Look, I know you probably think I'm lying but why would I contact you instead of just loading it all up and living the high life off the money I'd make selling it?"

"It does seem self-incriminating if you did indeed open this yourself." Deputy Wheeler nodded at him.

Nick moved to unlock the unit. "Maybe you can run a check on some of the packages for prints."

Deputy Wheeler and Nick entered the storage unit.

"Whoa." Deputy Wheeler guffawed. "You weren't kidding."

Suddenly, something slipped around Alexis's neck and tightened.

All she could manage was a garbled groan as she watched two men descend upon the storage unit. Slowly the world went black.

SIXTEEN

Alexis could hear shuffling as she woke up. The last thing she remembered was someone wrapping their arm around her neck and cutting off her air supply. She opened her eyes. The sun was bright. It took a couple of blinks before she could see anything. Nick lay unconscious next to the unit door.

She crawled to him. His chest rose and fell.

"Nick." She shook his shoulder. "Wake up."

Nick groaned and turned his head to her. His eyes opened to slits as he reached for his head.

"Are you okay?" She looked him over. He did not appear to have any serious injuries. At least not any she could see.

"Yeah." Nick's voice was gravelly.

Now that she knew Nick was okay, she needed to find Deputy Wheeler. Alexis stood and looked around. The police cruiser was still there, but nothing and no one was in the alley.

She looked in the storage unit and found Deputy Wheeler lying on his side. The drugs that once lined the walls were now gone. She raced to Wheeler's side and felt for a pulse. He had a steady heartbeat. Blood matted the back of his head. He'd been knocked unconscious too.

She shook him. "Deputy Wheeler."

He grunted and rolled onto his back.

Nick knelt down beside her. "He okay?"

She nodded. "For now. Looks like he was hit on the head. He needs to see a doctor to make sure there's no cranial bleeding. You both should."

Nick waved her off. "I'm fine." He rubbed the back of his head, probably where he'd been hit. "Are you okay?" His gaze traveled over her body.

"My neck is a little sore but I'm fine." She used her free hand to feel where the man's arm had been.

Anguish filled Nick's eyes. "I'm sorry. I should have protected you."

She shook her head. "There is nothing you could have done. There were at least three people. I saw two men enter the storage unit as a third was choking me."

Nick looked at her neck and anger flashed across his face.

"And now they have the drugs." Alexis waved around the unit.

Every time they uncovered something to help it was ripped from their grasp. Was this ever going to be over?

"Can someone make the room stop spinning?" Deputy Wheeler groaned and tried to sit up. Alexis and Nick helped him into a sitting position.

"Let me look at you." Alexis started to ruffle his hair, looking for the wound.

Deputy Wheeler waved her hand away. "I'm sure it's fine." He pulled his leg up and stood.

"Do you remember what happened?" Nick asked.

Deputy Wheeler rubbed his head and pulled back his hand. Blood covered his hand. "She made a noise, you got clobbered, I tried to fight off the attackers but one of them got a jump on me."

"Looks like they got what they came for," Nick said as she told Deputy Wheeler he needed to see a doctor.

"Cartel?" Deputy Wheeler asked, ignoring her suggestion.

Nick shook his head. "I doubt it. We're still alive. The cartel doesn't leave survivors. Who did you tell?" Nick's voice was strained as he stared Deputy Wheeler down.

"I didn't tell anyone." Deputy Wheeler held his hands up in surrender. "You called me about the drugs and I made an excuse to get over here."

"Come on, Alexis, we need to get out of here." Nick grabbed her hand and pulled her to a standing position.

"You don't really believe I had anything to do with this, do you?" Deputy Wheeler stood up.

"Nick? He was knocked out, just like us." Alexis wasn't sure why Nick was blaming the deputy. The man had helped them before and was meeting with them now. He was already going out on a limb.

"I don't know what to believe anymore." Nick squeezed the bridge of his nose. "Sorry."

Deputy Wheeler clapped Nick on the back. "I can only imagine what you're going through right now. I'll drive around to the office and take a look at the security cameras and see who got us."

"Unfortunately, they don't have them back here. You said things at the department have been weird. Were you able to pinpoint anything?" Nick asked Deputy Wheeler.

Deputy Wheeler's face hardened. "I haven't been able to find anything."

"I think there is someone in the sheriff's office that's helping the cartel. There've been too many close calls."

"No. All the people I work with are on the up-and-up."

"I used to think that too." Nick shook his head.

Alexis watched as Deputy Wheeler worked his jaw side to side.

"How well do you know the dispatchers?" Nick asked. "If you think about it, they knew you were bringing us into the station. And they knew you received a telephone call and that you were heading out somewhere. Wouldn't be that hard to call whoever they're connected with and have you followed."

"I just don't want to believe it." The deputy shook his head. "Get out of here. I'll see what I can find out about the storage facility and whether or not I've got someone on the cartel payroll in my office." Deputy Wheeler opened his cruiser door.

"Thank you." Alexis was grateful for the ally; maybe with Declan and Deputy Wheeler everything would turn out okay.

Nick pulled out his phone, pressed a few buttons and put the phone to his ear. They sat there for a few minutes. Alexis could hear the phone ringing on the other end. Frustrated, Nick hung up and put the phone down. He leaned his head back against the headrest and massaged his temples.

"Think," he whispered to himself.

Alexis grabbed his hand and squeezed. "We'll figure this out."

He pulled the car out onto the road. She looked out her window in time to see a car slam into them. Their car lurched forward and Alexis's body slammed against the door. Metal crunched and glass broke in her ear. The interior of the car filled with dust.

Alexis shook her head, trying to clear it. "Nick?"

"I'm right here." Nick's voice was strained.

The airbags surrounding her were violently torn out the window.

Hands grabbed her arm and began pulling her through the window. The seat belt cut into her shoulder, keeping her from going anywhere. She fought against the attacker.

A knife slid into her field of vision and her pulse quickened.

She screamed louder and fought harder. The seat belt was cut. Broken glass scratched across her side as her body was yanked from the busted window.

Her feet hit the ground and she scrambled for purchase, but it was no use. Her attacker was bigger and stronger as he pulled her from the wreckage.

"Nick," she screamed as she was dragged away from the car. Was he okay?

She scratched and clawed at the arms wrapped around her but to no avail. She was at her attacker's mercy. Where were they taking her?

"Alexis!" Nick tried to grab for Alexis's feet before they slid from view. He fought with his seat belt. Finally, he succeeded in freeing himself.

He opened his door and jumped out, intent on getting Alexis back. Nick made it around the back of the car. He watched as a screaming and kicking Alexis was thrown into the trunk of a car.

Two men he recognized as cartel members stood at the front of the vehicle with guns aimed directly at him.

"We want our drugs and we want them now," one of the men demanded.

"I don't have them." Nick fisted his hands.

"It doesn't matter," the man snarled. "You're a smart man. I'm sure you'll find them."

That was it. He didn't know who had them. They'd just been stolen and he had no leads.

"One hour. If you're not at the compound with the drugs, we will kill your girl."

The men climbed into their vehicle and sped off.

Hopelessness filled him. He had no idea who had the drugs. Obviously, it wasn't the cartel. So who had taken them?

What was he going to do? He pulled out his phone and dialed Declan again.

"Come on," he muttered. "Pick up."

He walked around the car as the phone rang. He could deflate the airbags but he wouldn't be able to drive it. The impact to the passenger's side had twisted the frame and front axle.

"Nick?" Declan finally answered.

"I need you now. They've got her," Nick nearly yelled into the phone as he jogged in the direction of the compound. He'd never make it there in time on foot but he couldn't stop and do nothing.

"Who's got who?"

"The cartel has Alexis. They want to trade her for the drugs." His heart ached for her. For more reasons than just that he felt she was his responsibility. At first, keeping her safe had been out of a sense of loyalty to Tony but now he'd grown to care for her.

"Where are you at?"

Nick could hear a commotion in the background. Good, maybe his friend was on his way. "I'm on Fir Street, heading north to the compound."

"Head to the storage facility. We'll pick up the drugs and make a plan for the exchange."

Nick gritted his teeth and shoved his free hand through his hair. "I can't do that."

"Why can't you?"

"Because they're not there anymore." Nick filled him in on the attack. "This isn't an exchange—this will be a rescue mission."

"Ten-four."

Nick kept a steady jog toward the compound. The wound in his leg pounded to the beat of his feet hitting the pavement. He pushed through the pain. Alexis needed him.

The memory of her kicking and screaming in the arms of Las Sombras propelled him farther.

A sedan passed him and slowed to a stop. Declan climbed from the vehicle. "What's the plan?"

"I don't know yet. I just know I have to get her back." He closed his eyes and went over the compound in his mind. The tunnel Alexis had shown him would have made a good entry point but it had been sealed. "Do you have any wire cutters?"

"Actually, I do. I keep a toolbox in the trunk. You never know what's going to happen."

Nick paused a moment. Declan actually had wire cutters. "Perfect. I know how we're getting in," Nick said. That was the easy part. Getting to Alexis would be harder.

The drive to the compound was agonizingly slow. After what felt like an hour they arrived. Their feet splashed in the tunnel. The smell of damp earth filled his nostrils. He quickly cut the fence and made entry.

Declan looked around. "Which building is she in?"

Nick wasn't sure. "There are five buildings in the compound, one of which burned to the ground. That leaves four. The building in the center of the compound was used mostly for the drug trade. They'd unload the drugs and split them for distribution."

Las Sombras would usually cut the drugs with powdered over-the-counter allergy medicine. It would lessen the potency but increase the bulk amount and thus the profits. The building at the back was for machinery and supplies. That left two buildings. Those buildings were a mixture of offices and living spaces.

"They're probably keeping her in one of the front two buildings."

But which one? Their time was limited since the deadline was fifteen minutes away. They would be expecting him any minute with the drugs. Except he didn't have them.

The cartel probably anticipated a rogue rescue mission as

well. *Think.* He'd lived with these guys for a year. He knew them. Knew their thoughts and habits.

"She'll be in that building." Nick pointed to the building right inside the compound.

"Let's go." Declan started toward it.

Nick stopped him with a raise of his arm. "They're waiting for me to show up. I'm sure they expect me to attempt to get her without the drugs. We've got to be careful."

"Affirmative."

They inched their way closer to the building, keeping themselves hidden. The door to the opposite building opened and Alexis was pushed out and toward the building Nick thought she'd be held in. She tried to run but one of the men punched her, sending her to the ground.

Nick started to go after the man, but a hand stopped him. "They don't know we're here. Be smart. We'll get her."

Alexis was pulled to a standing position and dragged through the front door.

Nick and Declan made their way toward the building, guns drawn and down by their sides. Ready for anyone that would confront them. Right now the compound was quiet, and no one was milling about.

"I'll take the lead and you can watch my back," Nick told Declan.

Declan nodded and grabbed the door handle. Nick nodded that he was ready. Declan ripped the door open, and Nick walked through. Scanning everywhere for anyone with guns. There weren't any.

"Clear," Nick whispered.

Declan entered the building and the door shut behind them. Nick could hear a commotion up ahead. Was Alexis fighting her captor?

Nick motioned Declan toward the noises. As they got closer he could hear two raised voices. He couldn't make out what was being said but the voices were definitely male. Several gunshots rang out on the other side of the wall, followed by a scream.

"Alexis!" Nick raced to the door.

"Nick," Declan barked from behind him, stopping him from opening the door.

All of his training had gone out the window with Alexis's scream. He wasn't thinking about his safety, just about getting to Alexis.

Nick reached for the door handle and counted to three. He pushed the door open and then he and Declan entered the room, guns aimed. The room was empty except for a dead Las Sombras henchman on the floor, multiple gunshot wounds to the chest. Alexis was gone. He flexed his fingers then curled them into a fist and set his jaw.

"Let's go." He took off through the other door, disregarding his safety.

Alexis's head was spinning. Everything was happening so fast. She'd been yanked from the wreckage and safety of Nick's presence and thrown into a trunk. Dragged into a building only to be kidnapped by someone else. All she knew was someone burst into the room and opened fire, killing one Las Sombras cartel member, then heaved her over his shoulder before running out and shooting another man. She tried to kick herself free but it was hard to do when she was in so much pain.

They stormed through the door out into the open air. It was so bright. She was shoved into the back seat of a car. Her bound hands made it difficult to sit upright from where she was dumped on the floorboard. The kidnapper climbed into the front seat, fired up the engine and took off. She struggled to get in the seat correctly. Pain pulsed in her side. She squeezed her eyes tight, holding back the tears that threatened to escape.

She finally sat up and was able to see the eyes of her kidnapper through the rearview mirror. They were familiar. Who did they belong to?

"Who are you? What do you want from me?" She should be grateful to the man for saving her from Las Sombras but she still had no idea what his intentions were. Had she just gone from the frying pan into the fire?

The man connected gazes with her in the rearview mirror.

"Your boyfriend has something I want and now I have something he wants."

That voice. She'd heard that voice sometime in the last couple of days. Maybe if she could see his whole face then she would know who he was. She'd seen so many new people she wasn't sure who he was.

His intentions were clear. He was going to use her for bait or a trade of some sort. Chances were with everything that they'd dealt with recently he probably had no intention of letting her or Nick live. It would be up to her to save herself and keep Nick safe. She inched closer to the door, grabbed the handle with her bound hands and gave it a yank. The door didn't open.

"Child safety locks." The man's eyes wrinkled in the corners like he'd smirked.

That was okay. She had another idea. She raised her arms up and over the seat and brought them down to where her bound hands were at the base of the man's throat. She put her knee into the back of the seat, giving herself pressure and leverage to pull back and incapacitate the man.

One of his hands flew up and grabbed her wrists and started tugging. She fought against his attempts. The car swerved as he fought with her one hand. She pulled harder.

Yeah, he would lose consciousness and wreck the car, but that was a risk she had to take. Her life and the life of Nick depended on it.

The man slammed on the brakes, throwing her forward. Her face smashed into the headrest. Pain spiraled through her head. The violent shaking gave the man just enough freedom to grab her wrists and pull her forward, smashing her face into the headrest a second time. He pulled her hands from around his neck and shoved her into the back seat, reached over into the passenger's seat, grabbed something and turned to face her.

She stared down the muzzle of a gun.

"I can kill you now and still get what I need." His face was tight, and the cords in his neck bulged.

She could see his full face. It was impossible. She blinked rapidly, not believing what she was seeing. The police had said he was dead.

"Now sit back. Be still. And I'll let you live," Agent Blackstone spit through gritted teeth.

She'd seen him get shot and the text that said he was dead. She and Nick were wanted for his murder. Deputy Wheeler and Declan confirmed it. How had Blackstone been able to fake his death and fool everyone?

The pain in her head and hip beat to the rhythm of her heart. She leaned over and lay down on the back seat. She wasn't going to get out of this car unless he let her. She needed to conserve her energy. Maybe when they got where they were going, she could make a break for it. She'd be risking a bullet wound. But at this point, all she could see was a bullet wound coming anyway. Only that one would end her life.

"Don't worry. If Nick comes through, this will all be over quickly."

Alexis doubted Blackstone's idea of things being over

matched hers. He probably intended to kill them once he got whatever he wanted.

Blackstone put the car in Park and hauled her out of the back seat. He dragged her into a small house secluded in the woods and shoved her toward an old rickety couch.

"Sit," he barked.

His shove pushed her off balance, and she fell onto the couch, jarring her injured hip.

He pulled out his phone and made a call. "Answer the phone," he growled as he sat in an equally decrepit armchair and pulled the gun from his waistband and laid it on the armrest. He hung up the phone, set it on his leg and leveled a steely glare at her.

Alexis squirmed under his scrutiny. He had no intention of letting them live once he had what he wanted. She was confident in that. It was probably too late for her. But she could do something and keep Nick from meeting the same fate. She needed to wait for the right moment.

She needed to distract him. Get him to lower his guard a little. "Why?"

"Why not?"

"Tony trusted you. Nick trusted you. Everyone trusted you."

Blackstone just shrugged. "Their mistake."

"You killed Tony, didn't you? Why?"

He didn't respond.

Everything was falling together. "You sent Nick on a fake undercover mission and stole the drugs to make it look like it was him. You were going to use Nick as your fall guy all along."

That earned her an evil grin.

How long did she have left to live?

SEVENTEEN

Nick drummed his fingers on the steering wheel. How long did it take to look up a license plate tag? The seconds were ticking by at a snail's pace and Alexis's life hung in the balance.

Declan's phone started ringing and he answered on the first ring. He listened before turning to Nick. "The plate is not registered to the vehicle you saw but it is registered to a Lucas Wheeler."

Heaviness descended on him. Deputy Wheeler was the local law enforcement connection and had been playing them all along. He'd arranged to have the drugs stolen from the storage unit. His injury was a ploy to keep the suspicion off him. But if he had the drugs, why would he need Alexis?

Nick started the car. "Get me an address."

Declan entered the address into the GPS app on his phone. Nick followed the directions given by the robotic female voice.

The voice announced their destination was ahead on the right. Nick drove past the house. A small motor home was backed into the driveway and a man was loading stuff into it. Nick turned the car around and parked out of sight.

"Let's see what's going on before we make a move. I don't want to do anything until I know where Alexis is."

They sneaked up the driveway. Declan pointed to the back of the house. Nick nodded. He crept close to the motor home, using it as cover as Declan disappeared around the house. He peered inside, expecting to see Alexis but instead, he found the missing drugs.

Voices grew louder from the house. Nick ducked down.

"Are you going to answer his call?" a male voice asked.

"Not anymore. There's no need now that I have the drugs." It was Deputy Wheeler's voice.

How long had Wheeler been working with Las Sombras? Not only had he been covering his tracks well but he'd also been a convincing ally. Nick felt so stupid. He'd been so focused on his own issues and Alexis that he missed the signs.

"Aren't you worried about having a DEA agent on your back?" The first voice interrupted Nick's thoughts.

Deputy Wheeler laughed. "No, he's *dead.* He can't touch me."

The only dead DEA agents Nick knew about were Blackstone and Tek Ford. Nick had witnessed Tek's death and knew there was no way to fake that. That left Blackstone, a man he'd left alive. Whose death had seemed strange when he heard about it—a great way to create a manhunt for Nick. And Alexis.

"But Blackstone has connections to the cartel. That should scare you."

Nick's mind scrambled to understand.

"Another hour and I'll be long gone. Now enough talk. Let's finish loading up."

Nothing was said about Alexis.

Declan met Nick at the end of the trailer.

"One exit in the back. I counted three people I could see including the two that just went in. No sign of Alexis but I couldn't see all over the house," Declan informed him.

"Let's take them quietly one at a time if we can," Nick instructed.

"Ten-four," Declan said, acknowledging the plan.

A man came out of the house carrying a box. Declan pounced, grabbed the man from behind and dragged him to the side of the house.

Nick waited for the next guy and repeated the same takedown. Declan finished securing his man and pulled a pair of flex-cuffs and secured the man Nick had subdued. Nick left Declan securing the two men and went after Deputy Wheeler.

Nick walked to the front door, weapon drawn, and peeked around the corner. The front room was clear.

"Yo, Steve," Deputy Wheeler yelled as he turned the corner and entered the living room.

Nick raised his weapon and aimed it at center mass.

Deputy Wheeler started to reach for his weapon on his hip.

"I wouldn't do that." Nick stepped fully into the room. "Keep your hands where I can see them."

Deputy Wheeler brought his hands back up.

"It was you all this time." Nick should have seen it. He'd been too trusting, and now Alexis was paying the price. "Where's Alexis?"

"How should I know?" Deputy Wheeler smirked.

"Look, I'm done being a pawn in this game. It ends today. Tell me where Alexis is."

"Why should I help you? You've got nothing that I want or need." Deputy Wheeler cocked his head.

"Cooperation goes a long way with the DA," Declan said, entering the house.

"Don't give me that line. I know how this works. There is no leniency for me," Wheeler spit.

The phone in Wheeler's pocket started blaring.

"Answer it."

If Wheeler had already received and ignored a call from Blackstone, perhaps that was him now calling again. If Deputy Wheeler didn't have Alexis, then that left Blackstone.

Deputy Wheeler slowly retrieved his cell phone from his pocket.

"Answer it and hand it over." Nick held out his hand.

Deputy Wheeler swiped a button and the ringing stopped. "You're on speakerphone."

Nick took the phone. Declan grabbed Deputy Wheeler's hands and started to secure them behind his back.

"It's about time you answered the phone." Blackstone's angry voice echoed throughout the living room.

"Where's Alexis?" Nick barked.

"Ah, Nick Anderson. You figured it out. I knew you were a smart man." Blackstone laughed. "Well, sometimes."

"Tell me where Alexis is."

"You're not in a position to make demands," Blackstone growled over the phone.

He was right. As long as Alexis was in Blackstone's clutches he had the upper hand. "What do you want?"

"I want the drugs Wheeler stole from me and all the evidence you have."

Could he really give everything up? All the evidence would be washed away and Blackstone would more than likely kill them anyway. It was a lose-lose situation but what choice did he have? Alexis's life was in danger. He couldn't bear the thought of her enduring any more pain, physically or emotionally. He'd grown to love her.

He clenched his teeth. "Where are you?"

"Bring everything to 6258 Cedar Drive. I get the drugs, and you get Alexis back."

The line went dead. Blackstone had hung up.

Nick turned to Declan.

"Go. I've got this." Declan stood guard over Deputy Wheeler.

"Now would be a good time for you to call in some help." Nick clapped Declan on the back.

"I'll call in the cavalry and fill the brass in on everything that has happened and that Wheeler and Blackstone are behind everything."

"Thanks." Nick turned and ran out of the house.

Time to rescue the woman he loved.

204Alexis sat on the ratty couch and looked around the room. There wasn't a clock in here, but she estimated it had been about fifteen minutes since Blackstone had given Nick the address. Blackstone looked at his watch and then stepped over to the window and moved the curtain.

Had it been long enough for Nick to get here? She couldn't let him give in to Blackstone's demands. Blackstone needed to pay for everything he'd done. Fueled by the anger for all she had lost and all she still had left to lose, she jumped from the couch and charged the man.

"This ends now." She barreled into Blackstone, shoving him against the wall. Pain ricocheted in her body at the impact. They fell to the ground.

She stood up and Blackstone grabbed her leg. "You're not going anywhere."

His grip tightened on her ankle. She tried to pull free, but it was no use. He gave a hard tug on her leg that threw off her balance and she fell to the ground. Blackstone pulled her close to him, let go of her leg and started to reach for her throat.

She used her freedom to kick him with all her strength. The first kick caught his gut. He doubled over with a grunt. The next kick was to his face. He collapsed on the ground.

Alexis scrambled to her feet, unlocked the door and ripped it open. She ran straight into a strong pair of arms. They wrapped around her. She tried to pull herself free.

"Alexis, calm down." It was Nick's voice.

She stopped fighting and all but collapsed in his arms.

"You can't do that yet." He wrapped an arm around her

waist and ushered her away from the cabin. Several agents dressed in tactical gear raced inside.

Nick ushered her to safety at the end of the drive. "Get down." He gestured to the rear end of a vehicle. "We'll use this for cover."

She could hear loud shouts coming from the cabin. "He was armed. I think he dropped his gun when I tackled him."

"Relax. They know what they're doing. Did he hurt you?" He started untying her hands.

"Right now, everything hurts. I'm not sure what's new and what's not." She had dried blood on her arms from the car wreck. She was afraid to look in the mirror to see what her face looked like. Probably more blood and bruising from smashing her face into the car seat.

"Once the scene is secure, an ambulance will come in and check you out." He placed both hands on her cheeks and stared intently into her eyes. "I'm so glad you're okay. I was so worried not knowing where you were or if you were okay."

"I'm okay now that you're here." She was suddenly aware of how warm his hands were. The warmth spread down her neck and stopped at her heart.

She wanted to kiss him and she guessed he felt the same because his gaze dipped to her mouth. She leaned in a little, giving him permission. He closed the distance. His warm breath caressed her lips.

"Anderson," a commanding voice boomed from the cabin.

Nick dropped his hands as if she was on fire and he was going to be burned. He stood up and faced the voice. "Yes, sir."

"Blackstone is secure. EMS is coming in."

Nick nodded and held out his hand for her. She didn't take it, but instead chose to rise on her own. He looked wounded and started to say something, but the ambulance pulled up. He rubbed the back of his neck.

"Let's get you checked out."

She walked past him and met the paramedics at the back of the ambulance. Nick followed, but didn't get in the way. The EMTs began to check her vitals and tend to her wounds.

A man strode up to Nick and clapped him on the back. "We got him."

Nick nodded.

"We need to debrief."

Nick looked at her and raised his eyebrows like he was asking her permission. He was a grown man; he didn't need her permission. He'd almost kissed her. And she'd almost let him. But then they'd been interrupted.

She watched Nick walk to a vehicle and start talking with a man whose stance screamed power. The disinfectant stung as the paramedics tended to her wounds. She kept her gaze trained on Nick. He and the man in charge were in deep discussion. It would seem whatever happened while she was with Blackstone, the powers that be had finally discovered Nick wasn't a bad guy after all.

He would get his life back on track, and she would do what? Go back to her cabin? She couldn't do that. The cabin was tainted now.

She had thought maybe there was something worth exploring between her and Nick, and maybe he even felt the same way. But the speed in which he had separated from her when his name was called told her he had no intention of pursuing anything with her. She'd opened her heart and thought maybe she could love again.

Nick and the man in charge talked a little longer, then they shook hands and Nick strode back to her.

"I've got some loose ends to tie up. Will you be okay to go to the hospital alone?"

Fear seized her. Yes, Blackstone was in custody. But that

still left the cartel and whoever had stolen the drugs. All of which had put a target on her back.

Despite the coldness starting to grow between them, she felt being with Nick was the safest place to be. "I want to go with you."

He shook his head. "Go to the hospital, get checked out. You'll be safe."

"You don't know that I'll be safe. The cartel is still out there and so is whoever stole the drugs. Someone got to me at the hospital once before."

"Deputy Wheeler."

Now he was trying to pawn her off on someone else. The mission was over and he couldn't wait to get rid of her.

"I don't need a babysitter." She stood up and straightened her shirt.

"No. Deputy Wheeler is the one that stole the drugs."

Her body stiffened. "But he helped us. He was with us when the drugs were stolen."

"I just came from his house, where he had the drugs packed in a motor home. He was working with Blackstone. I'm pretty sure he faked his injury at the storage facility," Nick said.

"Anderson. Get in your car and I'll follow you." The man Nick had been talking to slapped the top of his car.

"I've got to go. Get in the ambulance and go to the hospital."

"I'm going with you." She wanted to see this through. To see everyone behind bars.

"Look, I don't have time to argue. Just get in the car." He turned and jogged toward a vehicle.

Once the car was on the road, Nick pulled out his cell phone and dialed a number. "Hey, it's Nico. I found the missing drugs."

Her skin grew clammy as her pulse began to race. What had she gotten herself into?

* * *

"So the traitor calls and says he has the drugs. We already know you have them," Matthias, who was one of Las Sombras's enforcers, scoffed.

Nick rolled his eyes. "No. You *thought* I had them. But I found out who really has them. You want them back or not?"

The Feds were going to watch the handoff and then swoop in and arrest everyone. Between that and all the evidence Nick had, the cartel would crumble from there.

"Why should we trust you?" Matthias asked.

"You know what, don't trust me. I'll get rid of it another way. Line my pockets while I do."

"Now wait a minute," Matthias said, having a change of heart.

Nick spit out Deputy Wheeler's address. "If you're not there in twenty minutes I'll just help myself." He hung up.

"What's going on?" Alexis asked from the passenger's seat.

"What?" Nick focused on dialing Declan's number. Declan needed a warning that they were coming.

"Why did you just call the cartel and tell them you had the drugs?" Alexis asked.

Declan's phone continued to ring.

"We're going to bring the cartel down. Now." Nick took his eyes off the road long enough to look at her.

An automated voice informed Nick that Declan's voice mail was not set up. He slammed the phone down.

"The Feds gave me a wire and they're listening in. Once the cartel has the drugs, they'll swoop in and make arrests." Nick turned onto the road that led to Deputy Wheeler's house. "Stay here."

She started to object but he gave her his most serious agent face. "Stay in the car."

"Fine." She crossed her arms over her chest.

Nick slammed on his brakes, almost past the house. The motor home wasn't in the driveway.

"No. No. No." He shoved the car in Park and jumped out.

"Declan!" Nick raced for the house and burst inside. Declan lay on the floor in the living room, a crimson stain across his abdomen.

"Declan." Nick knelt down and felt for a pulse. A weak one beat beneath his fingers.

He needed to call for help but he left his phone in the car.

"Declan." Alexis gasped behind Nick.

"We need an ambulance," Nick shouted into the mic of his hidden listening device.

"Declan, can you hear me?"

Nick pulled Declan's shirt up and searched for the wound. A single gunshot wound to the abdomen. He ripped Declan's shirt and used the scraps to apply pressure to the wound.

Declan groaned and opened his eyes. "Nick?"

"The one and only."

"Here." Alexis knelt down and moved Nick's hand from the wound. She did a quick inspection before stuffing some of the cloth into the wound and then placing her coat over it. "Hold pressure and help me roll him up so I can check for an exit wound."

Declan yelped in agony at the movement.

"Okay, set him down. There is no exit wound." Her face was grim.

"What are my chances, Doc?" Declan looked at her.

She smiled and patted his shoulder. "Paramedics will be here soon. They'll get you to the hospital and get you all fixed up." The look on her face did not match the tone of her voice or the words she spoke. It was bad.

"What happened?" Nick asked. Where were the Feds? What was holding up the ambulance?

"One of those guys got the jump on me. He shot me and freed the other two and they took off."

Squealing tires followed by two car doors slamming sounded from the front yard. Finally, help arrived.

"Nico," Matthias sang as he walked into the house.

That's why backup hadn't arrived. They must have seen Matthias and his crew coming.

"Trust me and play along." Nick looked from Declan to Alexis before standing up.

"Nico, where's the drugs, man?" Matthias looked around the room before settling his gaze back on Nick.

"Deputy Wheeler put up a fight, shot my boy here and took off." Nick prayed that they would believe him.

Matthias looked at him skeptically. "You expect me to believe that?"

Nick gestured to Declan's wounded body on the floor. "How else do you think he got a gunshot wound?"

"Happened about five minutes ago, man," Declan said.

"We can catch him. What are we waiting on? He's got a motor home. The drugs are stashed in it. He was packing to make a run for it. We've got to go now. The paramedics are on their way and the cops probably aren't too far behind." Nick turned to Alexis. "Keep pressure on that wound until they get here."

"No. I don't think so." Matthias grabbed Alexis by the arm and pulled her to a standing position. "She's going with us, in case this is some sort of a trap."

Nick's stomach quivered. Alexis had panic all over her face.

"But someone has to stay and help my guy." He could not let her go with them. She had to stay where it was safe.

"He's not Las Sombras. What do we care? Now let's go."

"Go," Declan said, "I'll be fine."

He had grown paler since Nick had arrived. Nick wasn't sure he'd be okay.

"Go," Declan said again, more forcefully.

Nick followed Matthias as he shoved Alexis out of the house and to their waiting car.

"Let her ride with me." Nick had to keep Alexis out of the cartel car.

"Nope. As a matter of fact, you could ride with us too," Matthias said.

Nick didn't like that idea but it was better for him to be in that car with her than for her to go alone.

They all piled into the car as Matthias made a phone call. "Get the word out. We're looking for a motor home with—" Matthias looked at Nick through the rearview mirror.

"It's white with a black stripe all the way around. The door is brown," Nick said, describing the motor home.

"Tell them if they see it to let us know. We'll head out of town. Deputy Wheeler has probably split town," Matthias told his buddy on the phone.

If Nick were in Deputy Wheeler's shoes, he would do the same thing. Nick needed to think of a plan to keep Alexis safe. The Feds were tracking his phone and they were listening in on the body device. They would know wherever they ended up. It was what would happen before the Feds could storm in that worried Nick.

EIGHTEEN

Alexis didn't know what was going on anymore. They'd gone from one dangerous situation to another. Nausea roiled in her stomach.

Alexis gasped. "I'm going to be sick."

"Swallow it down, sweetheart, because we ain't stopping until we find the drugs," the driver said.

"Come on, man. She's squeamish and just dealt with all that blood." Nick covered for her. He'd seen her hold herself together before. He wanted her out of the car and away from danger.

A phone chiming interrupted the conversation. The driver put the phone to his ear.

"Yeah." He listened. "We'll head that way."

He put the phone down. "Looks like your guy was right. Some fellas found our motor home. It's heading east on the highway." The driver looked straight at her. "You might get to live after all."

A shiver rolled down her body.

The driver pressed the accelerator and sped past multiple cars. He took a series of turns, sending the car's occupants violently shaking through the car. "We're going to head him off and stop him."

"Where did they say they spotted him?" Nick asked, leaning up.

"They said he's by the old sawmill."

"What's the plan?" Nick asked.

She knew the Feds were listening in. Nick was trying to give them as much information as he could.

"The plan is to stop that motor home and get our drugs back." The driver sounded annoyed.

"How many guys are coming to help?"

"You're full of questions today." The driver eyed him skeptically through the rearview mirror.

"I've been through a lot recently. I'm just trying to determine what I'm going to have to do."

"You mean how many people you are going to have to stab?" Matthias asked.

"That was self-preservation. I knew you two were going to kill me. I kinda like living. I could have aimed for his heart," Nick said.

Matthias harrumphed.

"Don't forget I found the drugs and called you guys. If I wasn't loyal to the cartel I'd be halfway to Canada by now." Alexis realized that Nick was playing the bad guy. They were safe as long as they believed he really was part of the cartel.

"We'll have as many as we need and you'll do what you have to get our drugs back or Deputy Wheeler won't be the only one disappearing today."

Nick nodded, leaned his head back against the car seat, and closed his eyes.

They were on their way to more than likely kill a man, and he was going to take a nap? Alexis watched the scene racing past her window. The anxiety grew with each mile marker they passed.

The driver slowed and parked the car across the two-lane highway. A couple more cars pulled up and angled themselves, creating a blockade across the road.

Men armed with guns exited from the cars and got ready.

"Come on, Nico. Let's get our drugs back." The driver stepped out of the car.

Nick turned to her. "Stay in the car."

"Where else would I go?"

"As soon as everyone is occupied, I want you to quietly slip out of the car and run to the forest line." He nodded behind her.

"What about you?" She didn't want to leave him alone.

Nick reached out and cupped her cheek. "I will be fine as long as I know you're out of harm's way. I won't be able to focus unless you're safe." He studied her face. His hand was warm and his touch gentle. He stared at her with such affection.

"Alexis, I lo—"

"Here comes the motor home," someone yelled.

"Now, Nico," the driver yelled.

Nick dropped his hand. "Promise me you'll run to safety."

She nodded.

He opened the door and disappeared into the foray of gunmen. Was he going to say he loved her? Could he possibly love her?

Part of her still felt like she didn't deserve his love. And maybe she always would. But for the first time since Tony's death she saw the promise more than the problem. She loved him too. He kept coming back for her. Yes, he was focused on the cartel and clearing their names but he never pushed her to the side.

She looked out the window. Men stood with guns aimed at the approaching motor home. Unfortunately, it didn't appear that Deputy Wheeler had any intention of slowing down.

Lord, keep us safe.

"Don't shoot!" Nick yelled.

"What do you mean?"

"We need him alive. What if he dumped the drugs? If he's dead, we'll never know where they're at. Remember, he had two guys with him earlier." Nick was trying to keep the peace.

The motor home started to slow as it approached the blockade. Was he giving up? Her heart beat frantically.

It didn't matter. Everyone was busy. Now was an excellent time to escape. She slipped from the car and backed toward the forest line, keeping her eyes on the action in front of her. She searched the crowd of men looking for Nick, but he was nowhere to be seen. The motor home continued at a slow speed. This would all be over soon. She needed to run.

Now. She ran behind the row of cars. Yelling ensued. She couldn't make out what was being said or by whom. She stopped long enough to see what was going on. Men were surrounding the motor home, reclaiming their property.

Cars that drove up to the blockade immediately turned around and drove off, not wanting to be a casualty of whatever was going on in the streets. Maybe if she could get to one of those cars she could escape with them. In the distance, several dark SUVs with flashing red-and-blue lights came toward them.

The cavalry was coming. The cartel members rushed around and climbed into their cars, trying to escape before the cops showed up. She searched the crowd for Nick but couldn't find him. He'd catch up later; she needed to get to safety and let him do his job.

She turned and ran straight into a strong chest.

Arms encircled her. She started to scream but a hand was put over her mouth.

She looked up and stared into the face of the driver.

"Not so fast. We're not done with you."

He spun her around and wrapped an arm around her tightly. Hot metal was pressed against her temple. She squeezed her eyes shut as her body trembled.

Lord, I'm not ready to die.

* * *

The Feds were bearing down on them. The end was in sight. Nick needed to find Alexis and make sure she didn't get caught up in the takedown.

Only when she was safe would he then finish telling her he loved her. He once believed he didn't deserve her returned affections but now he knew better. He hoped she felt the same. The fear of her leaving him had died. He knew she would stay. All that could be sorted out later.

Tires squealed and a car narrowly missed hitting him.

"Nick!" Alexis's voice filtered to him through all the commotion.

He searched for her. Las Sombras were running scared. Hopping into cars and speeding off. *Lord, please don't let her be in one of the fleeing cars.*

Was she lying injured somewhere?

A scream erupted from his left. He whipped his head in that direction and caught a struggle at the edge of the road. Matthias had one arm wrapped around Alexis and the other holding a gun to her head. They backed into the tree line. Nick couldn't let her disappear.

He took off at full speed, speaking into the listening device in his shirt pocket. "If you can hear me, I've got one suspect dragging a civilian into the forest. I'm in pursuit."

He hoped the Feds were still monitoring the mic.

He entered the forest, and wood splintered on the tree next to him. Nick ducked behind another tree.

"Don't follow us," Matthias yelled.

"You're not going to get away," Nick replied. "The Feds are here. Just give yourself up."

Nick listened for snapping of twigs or crunching snow. He needed to know which direction they were headed. Getting Matthias to talk would help.

"If you cooperate, I'm sure you can get a deal."

"Not a chance." Matthias's yell came from Nick's right.

Nick peered around the tree. Matthias dragged Alexis backward through the trees, using her as a shield. Nick couldn't risk shooting and hitting her. He slowly crept toward them, using trees as cover.

"Don't come any closer. I'll shoot her." Matthias's voice held a tinge of panic.

While Nick didn't doubt Matthias would shoot Alexis, he doubted he would do so now. Right now, she was the only thing keeping him alive. But Nick also couldn't take the chance that Matthias was backed into a corner and willing to do anything to get away.

"Nobody has to get hurt. We can work this out." Nick tried to reason with Matthias. He needed to deescalate the situation.

Matthias stopped pulling Alexis and jammed the gun to her temple. Alexis whimpered.

"Just let her go." Nick stood close to a tree, angled so he could see Matthias but still had cover should he choose to shoot. Nick wasn't a negotiator. He didn't know if he could talk Matthias into giving up. Nick was afraid this was going to end in bloodshed. He just prayed Alexis wasn't a casualty.

Alexis yelped as Matthias jostled her, aimed his gun at Nick and fired multiple shots. Nick dived behind the tree. He couldn't shoot back and risk hitting Alexis.

The shooting stopped and Nick cautiously peered around the tree. Matthias and Alexis were on the move again.

"Suspect is headed north," Nick said, speaking low into his mic. He wanted the Feds to know which way they were headed, but he didn't want Matthias to know he had communication with them.

Alexis lost her footing and stumbled a bit, giving Nick a split-second opening to Matthias but it wasn't long enough to shoot before Matthias yanked her up.

She cried out in pain. "Please, my back and side. I need rest."

Matthias yanked her harder. "You can rest when you're dead. If you don't speed up it will be sooner rather than later."

Alexis stumbled again and this time Matthias lost his grip on her and she landed on the ground. He was totally exposed. Matthias raised his gun and fired just as Nick fired twice. Fire sliced through Nick's chest before he fell and landed on the forest floor. He couldn't breathe. He gasped for air.

"Alexis," he gasped. Where was she?

Pressure built in his chest with each breath.

He tried to sit up, but the movement was too painful.

"Nick." Alexis fell at his side. Tears streamed down her face. She took off her coat and put pressure on his wound. Sharp pain reverberated through his chest.

"Alexis. Are you okay?"

She nodded and then looked over her shoulder. "We need help!" Desperation filled her voice.

He reached up with a hand and touched her cheek. "I—"

He tried to take a breath but it was useless. His chest was slowly being constricted. No matter how much he breathed he couldn't get any air. His vision blurred as darkness creeped in. He didn't have much longer. He was suffocating. If he didn't tell Alexis how much he loved her now, he'd never get the chance.

"Alexis, I love you."

Alexis let out a cry. "Don't talk like that. You're going to be okay."

He closed his eyes and let the darkness win.

Alexis's chest constricted as Nick's head lolled to the side. "No." She patted his cheek. "Wake up. Please."

She looked wildly around the forest. "Someone help us! Please!"

Tears streamed down her face. Not again. She was losing another man she loved. “Nick, Stay with me.”

“Officer down!” Alexis yelled into the forest. That should get people moving. That is *if* they could hear her.

She patted his face, trying to keep him conscious. “You can’t leave me. I love you.” *Lord, don’t let him die.*

Crashing footsteps and loud voices carried through the woods. Help was coming.

“You hear that?” She talked to Nick as if he was still conscious. “They’re coming. You’re going to be fine.”

“Officer down! We’re over here,” she yelled.

Two men in blue windbreakers came into view. One with blond hair and the other with fiery red.

“Hurry,” she pleaded. “This is Nick Anderson. He’s DEA. He’s got one gunshot wound to his chest.” She told the blond as he knelt down beside her.

The other man bypassed them.

“Okay.” The blond man requested paramedics over his radio.

There wasn’t time to wait for paramedics to come to them. They needed to get Nick to them.

“He’s not going to make it. We have to carry him out. Tell them we can meet them and he’s most likely got a collapsed lung due to a bullet wound and is going to need a chest tube.”

“The other guy is dead,” the red-haired man said, returning to them.

“Help us get him out,” the blond man instructed as he grabbed Nick under the arms. The other man grabbed his feet. The two men carried Nick while she tried to maintain pressure.

A team of paramedics met them and took over and started to cut away Nick’s shirt to assess his wounds and prepare for a chest tube.

“We gotta go.” The ambulance driver started to shut the ambulance door while the paramedics continued to work.

"I want to go with him," Alexis said, stopping the door.

"We don't have the room. My guys need the room to work." The paramedic gave an apologetic smile and finished closing the door.

It was true. Nick needed a lot of help and she would just be in the way.

"I'm Agent Roberts. I need to get a statement from you," the blond man said from her right.

She started to argue with him. Nick may be dying and he wanted to talk about what happened.

"Let them do their job," the agent said softly. "I'll take you to the hospital. We can talk while we're waiting."

"Okay." She knew he was right, but it wouldn't make the waiting any easier.

Agent Roberts didn't push her to talk on the ride to the hospital. She was grateful for that. All she could think about was Nick.

The car was barely in Park before she jumped out and raced to the sliding glass doors of the emergency room.

"Are you here to see a doctor?" a young woman asked from the triage desk.

"A DEA agent was brought in a few minutes ago. Nick Anderson. What's his status?"

"And you are…?" the woman asked.

"My name is Alexis White."

"Are you family?" The woman tapped on her keyboard.

Of course, a privacy policy would prevent her from finding out his condition.

"It's okay," Agent Roberts said, showing his badge. "He was shot in the line of duty and brought in. We can wait while you call who you need to call." He tenderly touched Alexis's elbow.

Alexis whipped her head at the agent. She didn't want to wait. Was Nick still alive?

"Do you perhaps have a private waiting room or doctor's consult room? We're just the first of a long line of FBI and DEA agents that will be coming in on this." He didn't clarify that she was just a civilian and she wasn't going to be the one to offer that information.

"Of course." The nurse's demeanor changed from guarded to compassionate as she gave them directions.

Alexis let Agent Roberts lead the way to a room that held several chairs and a few end tables in clusters and a large television hung on the wall. He led her to a corner area out of the way. It offered a semblance of privacy while leaving plenty of room for other agents to come and go if they needed to.

"Let's go over everything while it's fresh in your mind." Agent Roberts produced a notebook and pen from his windbreaker.

Alexis stared at the waiting room door, willing a doctor to come in to update them on Nick's condition. Was he even still alive? Grief clogged her throat.

"He's in good hands," Agent Roberts said softly.

"I know. But it doesn't make sitting here waiting any easier." She sighed and leaned back in the chair. "Where do you want me to start?" Maybe talking about the recent days' events would distract her brain.

"Agent Declan O'Neil has filled us in with as much information as he could when he contacted us. Why don't we start with your husband's death?"

Declan. How could she have forgotten about him? He'd been bleeding from a gut wound when they'd left him in the deputy's house. "How is Declan?"

"He sustained some internal damage from the gunshot wound. The doctors were able to fix him up. He's going to be fine."

Relief flooded her. She'd been sure he would die if they'd left him.

"Good."

She'd want to see him with her own eyes and to personally tell him thank you for all he'd done for them. She'd never be able to repay his kindness.

"Your husband," Agent Roberts prodded.

Alexis took a deep breath and started talking. She didn't know how long she sat there answering questions. Agents came and went, mostly waiting on news about Nick.

A doctor knocked on the open door. "For Agent Nick Anderson?" Other than exhaustion, the doctor's face gave nothing away.

"Yes, sir." Agent Roberts stood.

Alexis stood too.

"The bullet punctured his lung. We did surgery and repaired the damage. He's stable and in recovery. He's still sedated but you'll be able to see him shortly. A nurse will come to get you when it's time."

Alexis's knees buckled and she collapsed back into the chair. Nick was alive. Tears filled her eyes.

"Thank you." Agent Roberts shook the doctor's hand.

Alexis leaned her head back against the wall, closed her eyes and listened to the agents talk among themselves.

Alexis heard shuffling to her left. She lifted her head and opened her eyes. Agent Roberts resumed his seat.

"I think I had gotten everything before the doctor came in. Did you have anything to add?"

She thought about everything that had happened and what she'd told him. "No, I've told you everything."

"Okay." Agent Roberts tucked his notebook in his jacket pocket.

Now she had to finish the waiting game. Her leg bounced anxiously. She needed to see Nick with her own eyes. Confirm he was okay. She wouldn't be able to relax until she did.

NINETEEN

The mental fog was so thick. Nick could hear beeping and voices but he couldn't make his eyes open. He tried to swallow but his throat was so dry. Something warm squeezed his hand.

"Come on, Nick." A woman's voice filtered through the fog. He recognized that voice. Alexis. She'd survived. The beeping increased as did his heart rate.

"Please don't leave me." Alexis sniffed as if she'd been crying. He wanted to wipe away her tears but he wasn't strong enough to lift his arms. He felt something caress his face. "Do you hear me, Nick Anderson? I love you."

He had to respond. Had to tell her he loved her too. He worked his mouth and fought hard, forcing his eyes open. Alexis's face stared down at him. "You're awake." Her face beamed. She turned and left his field of vision. *No, come back*. He squeezed her hand as tight as he could; he was not going to let her go.

"Declan, he's awake."

Her face came back into view.

Declan's face joined hers. "It's good to see you."

"I'm going to get the nurse." Alexis tried to pull her hand free, but Nick held it tightly. She looked at him. "I'll be right back. I promise." He nodded and let her go.

"Welcome back." Declan patted him on the arm.

The room began to fill with hospital staff.

Alexis stood off to the side and let the medical team do their job. He wanted her beside him, holding his hand. He also wanted to ask her about what she said. Did she really love him?

He'd just have to wait until they were alone.

The doctor explained his injuries and prognosis. He'd be up and out of the hospital in a couple of days. Once the doctor was satisfied with his vitals, he and the nurses left.

Declan had disappeared in the commotion. It was just him and Alexis. He lifted his hand and reached for her. She pushed off the wall she'd been leaning on and walked his way. Her hand slid into his like it belonged there.

He looked into her eyes. "So—"

His throat was sore. He swallowed a couple times.

"Here." Alexis grabbed a cup from the roll-away table next to the bed and held a straw to his lips.

He took a sip, and the cool water soothed his throat. "Thank you."

She set the cup down. "You were saying something."

He was. A knock interrupted him. He didn't need this right now. He needed to talk to Alexis.

"Come in." He never took his eyes off her. Hopefully, this wouldn't take too long.

A blond man in a blue windbreaker entered. "I'm Agent Roberts with the FBI." He nodded to Alexis. "I need to get your statement while it's fresh on your mind. I've already talked to Ms. White and Agent Declan O'Neil."

"He's one of the men that saved your life," Alexis chimed in.

Agent Roberts nodded. "I was at the right place at the right time."

At the right place at the right time? Nick knew it was much more than that.

"Thank you." Nick held out his hand. The agent gave a hearty shake then took a couple steps back.

Nick walked him through everything, all the while holding Alexis's hand.

"We've got enough to bring down the cartel and everyone involved." Agent Roberts stuffed his notebook into his jacket pocket.

"What about Deputy Wheeler and the sheriff?" Alexis asked.

Deputy Wheeler had tried to make them believe the sheriff was involved but was he really?

"Wheeler is in custody and talking. We're still investigating the sheriff but right now it doesn't look like he's involved."

"Have you figured out how Wheeler and Blackstone got involved with the cartel?" Nick wasn't sure how two law enforcement officers could turn on their oath.

"Blackstone isn't talking. Lawyered up as soon as the cuffs were placed on him. Wheeler on the other hand hasn't stopped talking."

"What's he have to say?" Alexis asked.

Agent Roberts leaned against the door frame. "Claims Blackstone came to him and offered him money to look the other way and let some things slide. Looks like he got greedy and wanted to make more so he stole the drugs. Says Blackstone never said how he started with the cartel. Most likely the same way. Money can be a powerful motivator."

There wasn't enough money in the world for Nick to actually work for the cartel. Death and destruction followed in the cartel's wake.

"What about Stella Ford?" Nick wasn't sure how she would have gotten involved.

"Seems like she was in a romantic relationship with Blackstone and joined the business. Tek's death really solved two of her problems." The agent raised an eyebrow.

"Was she the one that shot him?"

"Everything is still under investigation but we think Blackstone was the shooter. He has sniper training and access to sniper rifles."

"They kept me alive to use as the fall guy." Nick leaned his head back against the pillow and sighed.

"But they've been stopped and you've been cleared. Now we just have to untangle all the lies." Agent Roberts straightened and produced a business card. "Call me if you think of anything else."

"Yes, sir." Nick placed the card on the rolling table next to his bed.

Agent Roberts left the room.

"So," Alexis said.

"So," he replied.

"You were going to say something before the agent knocked." She tilted her head.

"Right before I passed out." He looked at their joined hands. "I said something."

Alexis's cheeks tinged pink. "You did."

"Yeah."

Someone knocked on the door.

"Not again." Nick rolled his eyes. "Come in."

The door flew open and Declan wheeled in with an IV pole. "I'm back."

"I was wondering what happened to you." Nick smiled. Declan had been there when he woke up but when the medical professionals swooped in he disappeared.

"Yeah, I've had enough doctors and nurses for a lifetime. I thought I'd let you have all the fun." He wheeled up to the bed and stuck out his hand.

Nick shook it. "Thank you for everything, man."

"No problem. It's what we do." Declan leaned back into the wheelchair. "I saw the Fed leave. I guess you know it's all over. Blackstone and Deputy Wheeler are in jail and the cartel has been shut down. You'll be exonerated and back in the game in no time."

"Yeah. Maybe." He wasn't sure he wanted back in. He only knew he wanted to be with Alexis. "There's something I need to take care of first." Nick looked longingly at Alexis.

"Oh," Declan said slowly and started to nod.

"Yeah," Nick said.

"I'll just be outside." He backed the wheelchair up. "Standing guard."

"I appreciate it."

Declan left and shut the door behind him.

Nick pulled Alexis's hand and patted the bed with his free hand. She sat on the bed.

"So, about what I said in the forest."

"Yes." Alexis bit her bottom lip.

"I meant it." He gazed into her eyes.

She looked down at their joined hands.

"The last several days have taught me a few things. Tony had talked about his faith a lot. I could never understand how he could have such a strong faith in the middle of everything we've seen. How God could be in the middle of everything and working among the evil? But it's evident that God has been in the midst of everything in the last couple of days. He's put the people and the things we needed in our path at exactly the right time."

Alexis nodded. "God has been with us this whole time, hasn't he?"

"He has." Nick squeezed her hand. "I know you're probably still grieving and it might be too soon. But I'm willing to wait as long as it takes."

He needed to get his feelings out there so she knew. He'd heard her say she loved him. Had it been just because she thought he was dying or could she feel that way knowing he was going to live? There was only one way to find out.

"Alexis White, I love you."

"I love you too." She smiled the most beautiful smile he'd seen.

Warmth spread from this chest to his extremities and his body felt light. He pulled her close. "I want to kiss you," he whispered.

"I want you to kiss me." She took control of the moment and closed the distance, her lips on his.

He was grateful to God for bringing her into his life. She proved that not all women were like the few exes he had in the past, who would run away when things got tough. No. Alexis stayed, even in the danger. She proved he could be loved even in the hard things.

Alexis lost herself in the feel of Nick's lips on hers. She let go of all the negative thoughts that had been holding her back. Nick had shown her she could be loved again. The last few days proved to her that Nick may be focused on his job but she would always come first.

She pulled back and stared at Nick. He tucked a strand of hair behind her ear. "What are you thinking?"

"I'm thinking Tony had been right that night."

Nick cocked his head. "How so?"

"He'd said God would take care of everything and He did. It hadn't been in the way I had wanted but it was in the way God had planned. Not just the day of the accident but every day since."

Nick nodded. "I agree. I've seen what Tony has been talking about all along and I understand."

She inhaled deeply. God had worked in Nick's spiritual life just as he had his physical life.

"Are you okay?"

She was more than okay. She felt weightless, like she could float off.

"I'm great."

Everything happened for a reason. Had they not been through the last year, would Nick have believed?

"So, it's not too soon for us then?" Nick asked.

She shook her head. "This feels right. I thought I'd never have another relationship after Tony. I loved Tony and I spent the last year blaming myself for his death."

"It wasn't your fault." Nick squeezed her hand.

"I think I knew that deep down but still blamed myself." The guilt had eased after her time with Blackstone in the cabin. "It wasn't your fault either. Blackstone and Stella had planned all this for a long time. Kill Tony, steal the drugs and let you take the blame for everything."

Nick's features softened and he exhaled. He must feel the same relief she had.

"My life and love with Tony is my past and I need to start looking toward the future." A future that didn't revolve around bringing down the cartel and proving to herself she wasn't responsible for his death. "Making a life without him. I'll never stop loving him but my time with him is over. I'll never get more time with him. It's taught me to cherish everything because tomorrow isn't guaranteed."

"I hope I'm included in your future." Nick squeezed her hand again.

She smiled. "It does. Including you in my future is right in a way that's unexpected but so perfect. It's only right because it's you." She was sure Tony would approve. He'd want her to move on and he'd be pleased to know it was with a man he knew and respected.

Nick pulled her close, wrapped his arms around her and held her.

"I'd be lying if I told you I wasn't scared about the future though," she said.

Everything was perfect right now. They knew who killed Tony and the criminals would pay.

"Things seem too right, right now. I feel like something

is going to happen and rip everything away." Heaviness started to fill her chest.

"Life and love aren't perfect. There will be ups and downs. Good times and bad times. But whatever happens, we will face it together. You and me." Nick rubbed his hand up and down her back. "I promise."

She looked at him. Really studied his face. He meant what he said. He would stick with her through it all.

Her heart fluttered. She leaned up and pressed a kiss to his lips. Her back twinged and she grimaced.

"Is everything okay?" Nick's brow furrowed.

"It's my back." She pulled herself free and sat up straighter. "I'm not sure I'll ever be one hundred percent."

"And that will be okay. You're perfect and I love you just the way you are." He pressed a kiss to their joined hands.

A knock erupted from the door before it was slowly pushed open. Declan wheeled back in.

"Sorry. I did the best I could but the nurse is giving me the stink eye. She said I should be in my bed resting." He smiled. "I think I better listen. She's kind of scary."

Alexis chuckled. "She's right, you know."

"Yeah, yeah." He waved her off.

"Thank you." Nick nodded to Declan and stifled a yawn.

"You need to go get some rest and so does Nick. Rest is important to the healing process," she admonished them both.

"Yes, ma'am." Declan wheeled himself from the room.

She stood and stretched her back, rubbed her balled fist into her hip. "I'll go and let you get some rest." She faced him.

"You don't have to leave," Nick said. "Unless you need to do some of those exercises."

She pulled a chair up next to the bed. "No. I just needed

to change positions. I'm okay for now. Go to sleep. I'll be here when you wake up."

"Yes, ma'am." He grinned then closed his eyes.

She watched as he fell asleep. His breathing evened out and a soft snore escaped his mouth. She smiled. God had truly blessed her through everything.

EPILOGUE

Alexis pushed the snowmobile faster. She was racing Nick down the mountain and to the park. The loser had to cook dinner in her newly built cabin. It had been a year since the ordeal with the cartel. She hadn't been able to go back to her cabin. So, she'd had it demolished and had another one built.

Nick had healed well and returned to active duty. He promised her no more undercover operations. He wanted to be Nick Anderson every second of every day so he didn't miss time with her.

Their relationship had started slowly but now they were spending almost every weekend doing some sort of activity together. He'd come up to the cabin and they'd go snowmobiling or watch a movie. Then he'd go home and come back the next day.

She was ready for their relationship to go to the next level. She had a feeling Nick was ready too. He seemed a little nervous today when he'd suggested the race. It was not their first race for cooking duty so she was suspicious today might be the day he proposed.

She slowly veered to the left and went around a tree stump. She was half tempted to slow down. Take her time. So, she'd be stuck cooking, but if he was ready to propose she'd be making him wait a bit. Ramping up his nerves even more.

But she couldn't do that. To be honest, she was ready to become Mrs. Nick Anderson. She liked the way Alexis Anderson sounded. It would look great on a business card. She could do some sort of double-*A* calligraphy. Now that she was actively selling real estate, she'd be handing them out.

Trees and shrubs blew by her as she sped down the mountain. Her heart beat frantically in her chest. She'd not seen Nick since she'd left him in her wake at the top of the mountain. Maybe she should slow down, let him catch up. It wouldn't be a fun proposal if she beat him to the park and had to wait. She slowed. She maneuvered the snowmobile around small bushes and rocks, taking in the slowed-down scenery. It was a beautiful day. The perfect day really.

She strained to listen over the sound of her motor but couldn't hear Nick's snowmobile. Had she really gotten that far ahead of him? Or did he find a faster way down? The idea had her speeding back up.

She burst through the tree line at the bottom of the mountain and pulled the snowmobile into a parking spot. The park was empty. Coats had been hung on poles again this year, waiting to warm up the citizens. She slowly spun around, looking for any sign of Nick. A large hot pink cardboard sign in the middle of the park caught her attention. Big block letters spelled her name.

She followed the sidewalk to the sign. A beautiful purple coat hung below the sign with a smaller sign that said Take Me. Purple was her favorite color. She shed her coat, unzipped the new coat and put it on. She dug her hands into the pockets, looking for what goodies Nick might have filled it with. A ring maybe?

She pulled out a granola bar, a five-dollar bill and a folded piece of paper. She unfolded and read it: "Turn around."

She took a deep breath and tried to steady her beating heart. Slowly she spun around and opened her eyes and her hopes deflated. Nick wasn't there. Where was he?

Her cell phone started to ring from her pocket. She pulled it out and Nick's profile contact lit the screen. She pulled her glove off and swiped the answer icon.

"Nick, is everything okay?"

No one answered. Just silence.

"Nick?" Had he had an accident?

Someone tapped her shoulder.

She spun around expecting to see someone but there wasn't anyone.

"Down here," Nick said.

She looked down. He was on one knee, holding a velvet box.

"You sneak!" she said, shoving her phone in her pocket.

"Well, I can't put a ring on your finger if it's wearing gloves."

"True."

"Shh. I'm trying to propose." Nick winked at her.

"Right." Alexis clamped her lips shut.

"Alexis White, will you marry me?" He opened the box and revealed a solitary diamond.

"It's about time." She stuck her hand out and spread her fingers.

"I guess that's a yes." Nick beamed.

"Duh."

He slid the ring on her finger, stood, picked her up and spun her around. "I love you."

"I love you too. Now kiss me." She lowered her head and their lips met.

The last year had been a year of healing for both of them. Not just physically but emotionally. They'd let go of their guilt over Tony's death. There were conversations about their relationship and the fears they each had had about falling in love again.

With the past where it belonged behind them, she was excited to start this new life with Nick and she thanked God every day He'd brought him into her life.

* * * * *

Find strength and determination in stories of faith and love in the face of danger.

Look for six new releases every month, available wherever Love Inspired Suspense books and ebooks are sold.

Dear Reader,

Thank you so much for choosing to read Nick and Alexis's story. I hope that you enjoyed their journey. Just like in their story, the real world is full of evil and hatred. But as believers, we know that God is at work in all things. We may not see it now but one day we will see God's providence in every part of our lives—the good and the bad. It's all for His glory.

Jennifer Pierce